I

Agent Provocateur

I

THE SECRET LIFE OF I

AN EROTIC NOVELLA

PAVILION

First published in Great Britain in 2007 by
PAVILION BOOKS
151 Freston Road, London W10 6TH

An imprint of Anova Books Company Ltd

Author: Trinity
Typesetting and jacket design: Lotte Oldfield
Copyeditor: Ian Allen
Proofreader: Kate Burkhalter

A CIP catalogue record for this book is available from the British Library.

ISBN 9781862057463

Printed and bound by MPG Books Ltd, Bodmin, Cornwall

10 9 8 7 6 5 4 3 2 1

This book can be ordered direct from the publisher.
Contact the marketing department, but try your bookshop first.

CONTENTS

PREFACE

In 2006 we published our first series of erotic fiction, *Secrets* and *Confessions*, judging there to be a huge gap in the market for sexy provocative literature, primarily aimed at women, which was neither smutty nor prurient, but instead revelled in erotic possibility and crafted its prose with care and elegance. The packaging was important too, as we wanted to create hardback books to be proud of and to display by the bedside, not grubby paperbacks to hide under the bed.

We were rewarded in 2006 when this collection of erotic shorts was announced the winner of the prestigious Erotic Award for literature.

Now we have decided to push the boundaries a little further with these novellas, which will allow the reader to begin a long journey with two enigmatic and liberated characters. The result is another pair of astoundingly frank erotic adventures which we hope stimulates the Agent Provocateur in you.

Joseph Corré and Serena Rees, 2007

PROLOGUE

WHO AM I?

I prefer to be . . . whatever you want me to be. Don't we all want to defy definition?

I can tell you a story – maybe more than one. I could vary them to suit your taste.

We all have a secret life. The screenplay runs through our mind every day. We record our own versions of how it was; we project our own scripts of how it will be, for an audience of one. Tonight I am going to lay myself bare: you will be my audience of one.

This is the story of me. You do not know who I am yet. Do you know who I could be?

Close your eyes.

Imagine me.

I know what I want and how to get it.

Age does not matter: but I am experienced enough to catch a younger eye; youthful enough to seize the heart of my peers; and still supple enough to inflame the older man.

I am neither tall nor small, but I am statuesque.

I am lithe and supple and blessed with bountiful curves.

I know how to dress.

I know how to use my naked body.

I know how to pose.

I know how to please.

I know how to persuade – with a poet's tongue or, indeed, with a whip.

It's all an act. It is an act of a play, on the stage of the body – in the theatre of the mind.

Close your eyes.

I

I AM YOUR OWNER

I can see you there!

Good grief! Who is this, who enters at this time of night? Who surprises me in the shadows?

Speak!

I am half-hidden, but the light on my soft skin will betray that I am half-naked. Very few know my secret, why I dress like this, what I do during the dark hours. It is better that way. Few would suspect that I am capable of parting a man from his soul as well as his fortune. But I cannot overpower a man in the soft clothes of a woman of propriety. I cannot ride my steed when I am shackled. I cannot subdue my quarry without the attributes of power.

Cat got your tongue? Tell me your name.

Revealing the whip will loosen it I am sure.

Tom, you say? Well, Master Thomas, you should leave now if you know what is good for you.

He hesitates.

Be aware, Tom, that if you take one more step there is no going back.

Will he run?

Still rooted to that spot? What exactly did you expect to find here?

I wonder . . . perhaps not a woman half-dressed in long leather boots and breeches. I must find the truth – why is he here? Flush him out.

But you knew I was here, Tom, didn't you?

He is staring at me wide-eyed. In amazement or fear? Perhaps both. Whichever, it will be easy to control this game.

I think you know very well what you are getting into. Admit it!

His cheeks flush. Is it experience or common sense he lacks? If it is experience, then that is something I can remedy straight away.

Come closer. Let me look at you.

His body is strong, tall and well built. Fine muscle definition shows beneath the cotton of his shirt. He is as dark as my stallion. His nostrils flare slightly as he breathes. His jaw is determined. I like this. I could have a battle on my hands. I could tear into him; I should discipline his obstinacy. But look more closely. His eyes are soft, yielding and nervous. He is still a boy at heart. I could wrap his youth tenderly in my arms, press a kiss beneath the lock of hair that falls over his forehead and . . . ? Set him free? Ah – but my reputation! No – I must enslave him. The discovery of my true identity cannot go unpunished.

Eyes down!

His eyes are on my breasts. They betray a hunger in him which excites me.

You have made some assumptions, Tom. I will need to correct them.

Let him look. Engage him with your body. You are beautiful. It is good to be appreciated for your beauty, not your power. It will help secure total obedience.

Do you think I should allow you to sully my body with your filthy gaze?

The tip of the whip now strokes him teasingly from navel to nipples, which stand proud under the fabric of his shirt. First up one side, then down the other. If the leather were not so softened with use it would scratch his skin as it floats over his neck, over his Adam's apple, over his lips. He looks me in the eye.

This stubbornness makes me angry. How should I punish this breach in my privacy?

Has he been sent to discover who I really am? I will teach him a lesson he will not easily forget. He can take his report home.

I would expect you to be more nervous, Tom.

I let the whip sting against his cheek and he jerks his head away to face the wall.

That is better.

He does not move again. Apart from a slightly faster, shallower pattern to his breathing, he does not draw back. No hand moves to touch the rising red stripe that begins to appear there. What resilience! He is controlling his rage. I can see the whites of his eyes. Look how imperious he is – I feel the rush of blood, a swell of anger. I am warming to my task now.

If you were my horse, I would quieten you now. Would you respond as sensitively as he does beneath me? Should I run the flat of my palm through your mane, over your neck, over the barrel of your chest, down your haunches?

I run my hand down his chest, over his navel, stop at his buckle.

You see I have tamed my beast, Tom. He is still a wild animal but he responds to my every command. He will take me anywhere I desire, at the mere suggestion of my body. He trusts me now, but first I had to break his will – he had a strong will, Tom – a will like yours.

I slide my hand down between his legs. Don't be deceived – he is enjoying this.

He knows when to stand still – for instance, when I am parting one of my wealthy fellow travellers from their treasure.

I cup my hand over the swelling beneath the cloth.

He knows to react immediately when I squeeze him between my legs . . .

He twitches.

. . . or spur him on. And, oh, how it exhilarates me

when we gallop if I press my cunt deep into the saddle.

His cock begins to strain beneath my fingers.

I think I am getting through to you, Tom. You seem to respond well. But I can see that I need to rein you in.

I loop the leather tail of the whip around his neck, and pull him into the darkened corner where the air smells of bare wood and horses. His breathing becomes comes long and hard. I can also smell a faint mellow note of liquor.

Did you need Dutch courage before you came? Don't be fooled. I know there is fear behind the defiance in your eyes.

His eyes are dark, penetrating, slightly agitated – familiar.

Ah! I have met you before. Indeed, I have almost you before! Haven't I, Tom? I saw the fear and excitement in your eyes then – before you fled with your mistress's purse.

You lured me away from her. And as I galloped after you the adrenaline flew around my body. My lungs filled with the thrill of the chase – my pussy rubbed against the saddle. You had too swift a start, were too far ahead, I would never catch you. I knew that. But it was too late to pull up – there was a new race developing between my legs.

You escaped me but the chase gave me more pleasure than you realized. All the more delightful for imagining what I would do if I caught you.

I did not guess then that I would have that chance.

But that is incidental. More importantly, Tom, I see through your imperious stance. It means nothing now. It is a sham.

The buttons fly easily around the floor as I rip open his shirt.

You are an impostor. I see you for what you are. Nothing but a common page . . .

I wrench open his belt buckle.

. . . for a haughty mistress . . .

I bring the belt whipping out from around his waist.

. . . who cares nothing for you.

With a sharp crack, I flick it out again against the tight, smooth skin of his bare chest.

You will not escape me this time.

His nostrils flare but he stands his ground.

Your first lesson, Tom, will be one of humility.

I remove the shirt slowly, appreciatively, peeling it back over the even, rounded shoulders. His back is tanned and toned. No stranger to hard work and fresh air. This bodes well. My pussy begins to twitch with potential.

Do I need to mark you with the whip again? Do I need to brand you? Will you escape again?

I walk around him, keeping the whip in constant contact with his body. He stares straight ahead.

I think not this time. But I will not tolerate

disobedience.

I lash the whip against his buttock. Again he displays admirable fortitude.

Down on your knees!

He sinks slowly, measuring his speed. His control is impressive.

Good – you learn fast. You will be rewarded for good behaviour.

I kneel in front of him and pull his face to my breast with both hands. He leans forwards eagerly and his tongue finds its goal. I wind my fingers into his hair and pull him closer. He sucks noisily at each nipple and the heat rises between my legs.

Then, not losing my grip of his hair, in a well-practised move, I throw my leg around his shoulders. He seems stunned for it is easy to bring him down on to all fours and mount him. Again, his acceptance of his treatment is stoic.

Good behaviour and endurance, Tom. Gather your strength. Find your balance. That's right. Feel my weight on your torso. Steady yourself.

I wrap my legs tight about him and squeeze my thighs, grip with my calves, pressing the leather of my boots against his sides. I hear his muffled grunt as tries to master his ribcage.

Oh, how I would like to crush your insolence.

I feel a powerful resistance below me.

Is that your anger rising? You will not unseat me.

Feel me settling down into you. If you try to throw me, I will break you.

He arches slightly, in defiance. It sends reverberations up inside me. He braces against my weight and we both wait, listening to his breathing. With each expansion, the entrance to my vagina is stretched a little. It is delicious. It begins to pulse. Each breath drives the throb further up inside me. My juices begin to well up around the entrance.

I should be riding you bareback, Tom – do you know why? Your spine is sheathed in muscle – the ridge of it fits perfectly against my mound. Do you know what that does to a woman?

I push myself harder against him.

Can you feel my pussy? Can you imagine what is happening to it?

I grip tighter with my legs around his chest.

Take a deep breath, then you will know. Yes that's good.

He is a good subject.

Now rock slowly, back and forwards. Yes, Tom, keep up that rhythm.

He rocks slowly with sure, strong movements.

Yes, like that. Keep it steady.

I grip harder and use my pelvic muscles to hold the magnificent dull ache deep inside my vagina.

It continues . . . intoxicating.

But I mustn't get ahead of myself – as much as

I would like to. See how a good pupil can distract his teacher?

I slide myself forward on his neck, bringing my legs over his shoulder, and fold my calves back beneath his chest.

There is another part of me that is aching for attention, Tom. Do you know what that might be?

My pussy rests against the crest of bone at the base of his neck. My clitoris swells agonizingly against this new torment. His arms tremble slightly under the added weight. He steadies himself. I feel him hold his breath.

Breathe!

I bring the whip back against him and feel his back dip slightly as the air leaves his lungs. He braces again – my pussy delights in the massage.

It's my clitoris, Tom. Do you know what you are doing to it? You are reined back into the centre of my womanhood. Did you know I could harness the power of your body while you are powerless? The power lies within me Tom – in my hottest, wettest place.

He snorts with the effort of sustaining me. I grab his thick mane in my left hand, pull his head up and push it down again.

Ride on, Tom!

I urge his body back and forth. Push him on with my hips.

Don't stop – you are gaining ground.

I force his head backwards and forwards, forcing the bone to rub against the growing focus of pleasure in my body.

Go on, Tom.

I am straining for release – I throw my head back.

Yes!

Euphoria wells up inside me, and an explosion of light fills my head. I am blind, Tom!

I need to catch my breath.

I must compose myself.

Let me bring my feet back along your back. No, I won't let go of your hair; I need to rest my forehead against my hands.

His strength is sapping. His body slackens and . . .

Did I say you could relax?

. . . he slumps (through shame or fatigue?), but still I hold his head up by his hair.

No, Tom, our exertions have only just begun. You see, I have always believed that one good deed deserves another.

I pull his hair and he is back up on to his knees again.

You have whetted my appetite – my clitoris may be appeased for now but my vagina yearns for more sport.

I stand behind him.

You may listen . . .

I pull off my boots, slowly. The sound of flesh sliding against leather always excites me. I place them carefully, side by side.

. . . but not watch.

I slip out of my breeches and throw them over the boots.

You may look when I decide . . .

I stand in front of him for a moment.

. . . but not touch!

I take a step closer to him, lifting his chin with my finger.

I need to examine you – for faults. I will punish each one I find.

I circle him, slowly, stroking his flanks with the whip. He stares at my pubic hair as I pass by. I press it close to his face and he involuntarily lifts his hands. I crack down the whip.

I said no touching! Hold out your wrists.

I tie them behind his back with leather straps and stand back to admire my handiwork.

What a magnificent sight he is in front of me. There is much life left in his body yet – his swollen cock makes that plain. His chest rises and falls with the power of an ox. His head is bowed but he is quiescent, not beaten. What next? I need to harness that muscle.

What should I do with you, Tom, after all that hard work?

I sit down in front of him. He is looking at my feet. Good boy.

You must be tired. Are you hungry?

I open my legs.

I will let you have a taste of what is to come. If you impress me you may win more freedom.

He is alert to every movement now. His body is primed – waiting.

Look at my pussy, Tom. See how I hold back its wet lips and slide my fingers deep inside me?

I pump my hand slowly in and out between my legs, spreading my own juice around the lips, over the clitoris. I can see his manhood straining at the cloth.

What are you thinking, Tom?

I begin to make silky circles around my clitoris.

I am wet, Tom – can you see that?

His eyes are fixed on my fingers. He takes a deep breath.

What are you going to do about that, Tom? Are you thirsty?

He stays where he is but nods slowly, emphatically, over and over again.

Well, come to me, then! No! On your knees.

He is here. Leaning forwards. I stretch my legs wide at his approach, then clamp him in place with my strong thighs.

Blow gently, Tom. Awaken me.

His breath is soft and warm – I hold my lips open for him, then let them fall closed.

Breathe deeply. Learn my smell.

His face is in my hair. His chin rests momentarily on my pubis, he lets his weight fall forwards and he makes small deliberate circles – it catches me unaware. I am momentarily detached from my duty.

Explore me, Tom.

He presses the bridge of his nose up into my folds then brings his head up slowly and down again.

Sweet agony. Yes. Yes.

His face is covered in my juices and still he nods. Up, down, up, down. My tension is mounting.

Taste me, Tom. Find the source.

He laps at me with a broad, strong tongue. He continues to nod. From back to front to back to front to back. The shivers spread from my thigh to my breasts. Each lick brings them home again.

Find my secrets. Learn where they are hidden.

His tongue is hard and questing. He locates my clitoris immediately, then draws a line back slowly to the entrance to my body and begins to trace circles around it.

Yes!

His tongue slips inside me and a frantic search begins.

I . . .

His lips follow, kissing, mouthing silent entreaties. Pressing, teasing.

I am . . .

I can bear it no more. But still he continues. His mouth conducts symphonies from me, beats a tempo only my body can hear. I am taut as a violin string, vibrating, humming. He only has to draw the bow and . . .

. . . aahhhh!

I become aware of the sound of my heart beating. I am lying on my back. My chest rises and falls heavily. My thighs are still clamped around his shoulders. He dares to throw a glance at me: I catch a glimpse of hope and . . . bewilderment? My heart softens.

Are you still here?

I smile at him. His head is bowed. It is time to surprise him with compensation for all his hard efforts. I sit up and pass my hands behind him to unbind him.

Now unleash yourself.

He thinks I cannot see but I know there is a smile somewhere just behind those lips. He hides it well. He is a pleasure to teach.

Still proud? Let's see if you are right to be so.

His cock is freed and springs heavily out of its prison.

What glory! I have found the cause of your arrogance.

His erection is magnificent – it begs to be caressed. Not yet. He slides his hands down to lower his trousers, shifts his weight on to one leg.

No, keep your boots on. I want your breeches around your knees. I want you shackled.

Although there is no reason for him to escape now.

I weigh his balls in my hand, watching his proud member salute in front of me. I encircle my thumb and middle finger around its base and tighten the noose with slowly increasing pressure. A glistening pearl forms at its tip and I spread it around the head of his shaft, using his own juices to smooth the path of my finger which now burns circles into his straining flesh.

What's that, Tom, still silent? We'll soon have you moaning.

I cup his tightening balls and stroke him as he grows to meet the tip of my tongue. I can taste the salt of his excitement.

Let me hear you, Tom. Encourage me.

I take his manhood in my mouth. He is hot and pulsating. I feel an increasing throb as I pull my lips over his ridges. He pushes his fingers into my hair, pushes my face closer, but I withdraw.

His slippery cock nods angrily.

Steady.

Oh, the agony before the ecstasy!

I run my tongue around his head – then suck down hard. I take him all. Feel him deep in my throat.

At last Tom finds his voice. I can hear him begin to moan as I move up and down him, closing my lips around him. Sometimes I am firm, sometimes so light he will hardly feel it. I keep him guessing as to what will come next. He begins to beg quietly. I nibble and bite him. I hear him gasp.

I take his balls in my mouth and suck them and lick them while I hold his prick in abeyance with my hand.

Come on, Tom, come on.

I let him fall back into my mouth.

Deeper and deeper.

He thrusts towards me but I dig my nails into his buttocks to keep him still. I *will control the pace.*

I bring him to the edge time and time again. I am careful not to spill any precious drop of him – not until I am ready.

I can feel him close now. I sit up. His cock dangles precariously in front of me, eager to be warm again.

Not yet.

I pull him down on top of me.

His long, rigid body fits into mine. I move around so the hardening bulge of his erection comes up tight against my clitoris. He shifts to try and find the entrance. But I grab his hand and push it down to me.

Not yet.

He strokes his hand eagerly over me, into me, out of me, through me. I tip my hips towards him to beckon him in further.

Deeper, Tom, deeper.

His fingers become stronger, more rigid. His thumb presses against my clitoris. It is still not enough. My clitoris is screaming for more – my pussy too. It has that deep pulsating ache which can only be sated by deep, extensive penetration.

I push my hands against his shoulders and press my weight down upon him. I turn him over, straddle him; place my cunt over his prick.

I need to feel you inside me. Fill me.

I slide myself down on him, feeling his girth, feeling him swell and push.

Fuck me . . . fuck me now.

I grind down upon him. He moves to hold my shoulders but I grab his hands and pin them down beside him. He begins to buck and thrust beneath me.

Yes . . . Harder, Tom, harder!

He pushes himself inside me with great force and I ride him with fury, sinking deep down upon him as he rises up inside me. I cannot breathe. I cannot bear it any more.

Tom, I . . .

Suddenly, I am unseated and he throws me on my back. I fight back but it is no use. He grabs me and tears into me. I am moaning with each thrust. Tilting upwards to meet him each time.

His cock begins to rub that very spot deep inside my cunt that few can find.

Don't stop. Don't stop!

His hands work into my hips – the fingers press rigidly down so I cannot move. And still he ploughs into me.

Oh . . . push harder . . . deeper . . . inside. Fuck me harder. Punish me!

He does. Then his mouth finds my breasts. A shot of flame travels through me.

I scream, I kick, I cry. The race is on.

Kiss me.

His mouth meets mine. He is rough. He is unstoppable. He is riding for his freedom.

Bite me.

I feel his teeth. My claws are in his back. His hot breath is against my cheek.

His hands are wound into my hair, pinning my head back. My cries empty out into the air.

Yes!

I wrap my arms and thighs around him and hold on for dear life, rubbing and straining for release. He bears my weight completely, thrusting inside me – this boy is strong.

He throws his head back.

I feel my body changing. The heat in me is rising. I am losing my senses – the blood fills my ears. I am blind to him. I am deaf to my screams. I grip him with my very core – squeezing the ball of fire up through my body –and the wave rips upwards into my centre through my heart up into the back of my throat.

Our sweat runs together. Our hearts beat together. We breathe together.

He is spent. He is heavy.

He sleeps.

I smile.

It is over, Tom.

I have tamed him – he is addicted.

You know who I am now. But you have tasted the pleasure and you will keep my secret.

And he will be back for more.

II

I AM A COURTESAN

I looked behind us. Not one of our walking party had yet appeared around the corner in the path. I turned back to face Kit, shocked again at how attractive I found him despite my low opinion of his romantic behaviour. I had the unusual feeling of being in the presence of someone who had the upper hand. He raised his middle finger to his mouth, touched it lightly with the tip of his tongue and raised his eyebrows. His beauty and his control of the situation did nothing to help me regain my breath. I tried without success to wipe carnal possibility from my thoughts.

I shifted my long silk skirts with determined hands. My eyes did not leave his. Gratefully, I felt the bones of my stays support me. My seamstress had done a wonderful job; thousands of tiny stitches supported the perfect fluttering cleavage. His gaze switched momentarily to the beauty spot that rose and fell on the pillow of my breast. His eyes returned to mine. I resolutely stood my ground. His words, when they came, were considered but not unkind.

'Do I have your measure? Perhaps your fortunes are fading?' He paused for effect. 'I know why you are here.'

Perhaps he did. It was the role of courtesan that our host, Mr B, wanted me to fulfil in the theatre of events he had meticulously planned for this 'convivial weekend'. My interrogator's suspicion was irritating, but it would not be of great import if I could persuade him to maintain a complicit silence. What stung was that he had perceived that, thus far, I had failed. My contract with our host was to allow the guest of honour to seduce me. Not that I had been a stranger to intimacy with the male body in the last twenty-four hours, you understand. Between my arrival and my chance to sleep I had been fortune to three encounters. I had been undressed by the eyes of the coachman who bore me to the front door of the Palladian manor. My sex had been secretly assaulted after supper, and under the card table, by the overenthusiastic toe of the Italian dandy (Signor L may have entered into the spirit of a polite house party, but was too stupid to realize that his gentleman's attire did not make him one). Finally, using a cleverly wrought headache, I had secured early retirement from the assembly, despite their protestations, but had been tiresomely interrupted by the midnight pleas of our host for the punishment of his prostrated buttocks.

It should be admitted that three hours of dull conversation, the creases caused by the molesting foot in a dress that had cost a small fortune, and never a look all evening from my titled quarry, conspired to allow the swift administration of that punishment some vent to my frustration.

'Was it your chastisement I heard as I took myself to bed?' he asked with mock sympathy, lifting a gentle hand to cup my face.

Had the wretch been stalking the corridor? The corner of his mouth twitched slightly. His thumb moved to my lips to stroke then rest upon my Cupid's bow. It suffused a soft warmth which opposed the bite of the cool morning air. I was angered but loath to pull away from genuine intimacy. I made to correct his assumption, but he stopped the words with immediate pressure of the offending digit. At last he leaned forwards. I thought he would kiss my lips but instead he whispered to them conspiratorially, 'Your mistress has been invited here to help our corpulent host win the reward of his patron. If she cannot use your beauty to ensnare his interest, how can she further her own?'

And with that he withdrew his thumb. It traced a bleeding line of rouge lip stain on to my powdered cheek. The heat rose in me now. I stepped angrily aside.

'If my face is my fortune, your clumsy painting will not help it.' He laughed a little and moved to wipe the streak away with the hem of his frock coat. I caught his arm. 'Nor, may I add, does your speech make the word "mistress" sound an attractive proposition.'

I detected the wound, and regretted speaking so sharply. We must have made an arresting sight – caught in courtly fashion, hand to arm in silent deadlock – for just then a woman, in dress more suitable for the autumn chill, exercising two dogs, crossed our path and stopped in surprise. She looked as if she might say something but hurried away.

Something of the tension between us was dispelled. We laughed. And when, as he dropped his pose, his hand brushed my breast accidentally I was swift to catch it there. My powers had not left me. I had earned his understanding. To reinforce it with the promise of reward I proffered an arch challenge: 'You assume incorrectly that if you address my lips so intimately you may also have similar access to the rest of my person. You may not, Sir . . . without proving your stamina.'

Noting the return of his smile, I quickly scanned the hidden track to my right, dipped beneath a low branch and took the first steps towards what I hoped would be a pleasurable diversion with one of the most striking men I had yet had the fortune to meet.

The alternative of another minute's walk in the company of either the daughter of our host, the stupid Miss B, or the overexcited Signor L did not appeal. Neither did I wish to meet my host again until some progress had been made with his gruff patron. So, lifting my heavy skirts, I increased my step to a giggling trot. Courtesans too can have their folly.

The ensuing chase covered the short distance up through the trees to a classical shooting lodge. Built by one of Mr B's most revered ancestors, it stood atop the hill overlooking the estate. A previous visit with Mr B had revealed a comfortable interior complete with fireplace, dining table and fur-strewn chaises. The chaise on the raised dais I knew well. It offered both comfortable accommodation and the added delight of reflecting its occupant in the panoply of mirrors decorating the walls. If one turned (or was turned) to lie on one's belly a magnificent view across the vale could be wondered at. It was a splendid idea. It would be an hour until the other guests arrived there by the scenic route. And with this man I was sure I would have no recourse to the view.

While I scurry up the path to pleasure, may I take a moment to paint a little background for you? Before you complain, your anticipation of my reward will make the final description all the sweeter.

It was now two weeks since the handwritten invitation had arrived at my door. I had known Mr B for two years. He took great pleasure in detail. I was used to his needs and thus my eye carefully appraised every word.

The letter offered a weekend's entertainment in polite company. The other guests, apart from Mr B's wife and daughter, would be an Italian composer, a Scottish widow, a young business associate and, it was his honour to host, his most revered patron the Duke of — (famous for his benefaction, and infamous for his predilections).

On Friday we should arrive for tea. After dinner there would be cards or conversation. Saturday would include a walk to the folly for lunch. The afternoon was open to any entertainment or rest. The evening would follow Friday's pattern. We were free to leave on Sunday morning. On the enclosed card Mr B had underscored the date: '17th April 1770'.

But I can see your attention wandering, so I shall return to my story. I had allowed myself the delicious girlish terror that hands would grab me before I reached my goal. I have now reached the folly door in a genuine scrabble for my safety. I am panting, hindered by my tight bodice, unused to carrying the weight of fabric hanging from my robe. My cheeks are flushed with excitement. My eyes are alive with expectation. Any moment now the door will reopen behind me. I lean back against it heavily, fearing that my slight frame is no match for his strength . . .

To my relief there was no immediate surprise. Perhaps I had a little time. I cleared my throat for composure, took a deep breath and moved to one of the many mirrors to repair my face.

The chaise longue was precisely where I remembered. Suitably, it was slightly hidden from view. I would arrange myself there. I would be in full command of the scene when my lover burst in. I sank back into the deep sable, imperious but not unapproachable. I closed my eyes. It would not do to appear expectant.

After a while came the reassuring click of the latch. The door remained open for a few seconds and then was closed, quietly. After an interminable silence, the weight of a male shoe clicked and scuffed across the sandstone. He was looking for me. I imagined him turning, surveying the opportunity. I controlled my lips. A muffled noise of surprise and approval revealed that I had been spotted. His steps towards and on to the dais corresponded exactly with my imagination of how he would approach. I feigned sleep, attractively.

I became aware of warm breath at my neck. The soft exhalations spread upwards towards my ear.

I perpetuated the myth of sleep. My nipples hardened against the stiff fabric of my bodice. I used the rise and fall of my breathing to tease them again and again against the resistant wall. As his lips brushed my skin they became taut captives beneath their cotton layers. A warm glow began its practised journey down the route from stomach to navel, tightening there with each touch of his cheek and nose as he pushed slow kisses into the nape of my neck. He had a warm smell of sandalwood of which I had not been aware during our earlier encounter. I breathed him in. The perfume pervaded my thoughts. As his hands reached to cover my breasts I allowed my senses to confuse his strokes with the thoughts of warmer climes, of spice markets, of overladen stalls spilling silks into the streets.

I began to swim in the reveries. It was only with slight pretence that I twitched as if half-drunk with sleep while his hands explored the boundaries of my bodice. Suddenly, he thrust his fingers below the fabric, rubbing four scorched furrows down my flesh; scratching my nipples on their return. The intruders retraced their burning tracks gently to firmly cup and lift my breast. I yielded slightly but immediately, arching my back just enough to be complicit in the act. It was noted. Firmly, with determined grace, he levered my body towards him whilst gaining sanctuary for his own on the couch by my side.

I affected repose, left hand abandoned by my cheek. My right began to feel the tightening cloth of his breeches, which betrayed the state of his cock straining a few inches from my fingers. My vagina responded with an ache which longed to sheathe his hardness. Yet I did not respond, nor did he expect me to.

He rolled closer to me and pushed his hardened self down into the cup of my hand that lay beneath him. With a little ingenious pressure of the fingers I could enrage him further without breaking my somnambulant spell. He began to pull up my gown over the many petticoats, returning rhythmically for each stray fold of fabric. What acts were we about to witness? He used his second and fourth fingers to pull back each layer. With assured patience each wave of slipping silk was accompanied by the steady progress of his strong middle finger as it travelled up over the tops of my gartered stockings and over the inside of my thigh. Then, using the same persuasive gestures, he began to pull at my undergarments until at last the flesh was exposed. His hand came to rest below my swollen sex.

There was a pause while the cold walls of the folly witnessed the unison of our breathing. He covered my mouth with his and plunged his fingers into the folds of my moistening crotch. My eyes rolled with the ecstasy of the moment. My drowsy eyelids parted and I saw the face, not of my lover, but of the Duke.

I was thrown into confusion – felt again the urge to squeal that had threatened me in my flight to the folly. My seducer interpreted the sudden movement to be 'the awakening' of his sleeping Venus, and he sealed each eye closed again with heavy kisses.

I regained composure of my body but my mind raced. At what point had the Duke come in? Who had lifted the latch? Was my would-be lover here in the same room or had the Duke entered instead of him? There was no way of knowing. And there was no question of stopping the inevitable as he heaved himself upon me and thrust himself inside. His left hand stroked the contours of my upper body. He turned my chin with barely restrained power until my head was thrust back into the furs and alternately bit and licked my neck as he extended deeper into me.

The heat of my seduction was now laced with an ice-cold realization. My mistake would be too easily understood if witnessed by our potential voyeur. The arrogance of my assurance would be on naked display. I was also strangely aroused, not by the groans of the man who was pulling himself roughly in and out of me, but by the bittersweet fear of being caught. My cheeks were burning now. My eyes sought desperately around the room but found no one.

What I clearly saw was a hundred reflections of our sport, magnified and reduced. Shockingly, many returned my gaze. An equal number looked away, oblivious, subsumed by the moment. All of them were being rhythmically bored into by the virile bodies of an infinite number of seducers.

My anxiety was matched by a visceral tide of excitement. I was being driven closer to orgasm in spite of my disengagement from the scene. I closed my eyes and imagined being both penetrated by another man and watched by one hundred more reflections of him at the same time. It was immediately overpowering. I abandoned my body and my thoughts to this fantasy as my sex contracted around my assailant. I felt his balls tighten and his thighs stiffen; he withdrew himself momentarily, eyes raised to heaven, nodding at his own arrival at the moment, then came in spasms accompanied by a long, low, animal noise, and slumped upon my shoulder.

As his head fell below my line of vision, and my eyes became accustomed to the bright light, I was just able to distinguish the back of Mr B, ushering his wife and daughter past the window.

I extricated myself from below the passive body.

'I think, Sir,' I said, patting down my skirts, 'that it is time for lunch.'

The lunch arrived moments later, borne in the

baskets of the excited walking party as they burst through the door chattering excitedly.

'Hello,' cried Mr B cheerily, winking at me whilst he spread the dining table with cold cuts and condiments. 'I saw you come just before us, my dear,' he added. His words were carefully rehearsed and full of joy. 'Have you by any chance seen the Duke?'

I raised a finger to my lips. 'I believe that we discover him at rest.' I gestured in the direction of the chaise. Mr B looked delighted and moments later the Duke appeared by my side, stretching theatrically.

'It's a fine building for this kind of amusement, old fellow,' he proclaimed. Our host looked as if he would burst with pride.

'Ah, your Grace,' bustled Mrs B, hurrying past me to retrieve my seducer by the elbow. She manoeuvred him to the table. He looked remarkably unruffled.

Mr B, having placed his guest at the head of the table, returned to me, hand outstretched. 'Come along, come along, everyone. We all need sustenance after all that exercise.' He gave me another wink. They were becoming tiresome. 'Come to the table!' He pulled me towards a chair.

The lunch passed without memorable incident; the conversation was tolerable.

I returned to the house with a very jovial Mr B, now on the wrong side of two very good bottles of claret, clinging to my arm. 'Well done, my dear,' he giggled repeatedly. 'Well done.' I felt a little relief at this, but the normal feelings of success were diminished by the knowledge that it was more by luck than gamesmanship that had allowed me to settle the contract.

I was exhausted. I took leave of him as soon as I could and retired to my bedroom.

I awoke in a darkened room to see a young girl crossing the foot of my bed. I sat up, confused. 'I have just drawn your bath, Ma'am,' she said, and left the room. I looked at the ormolu clock on the mantel. It was half-past five. Perfect. An hour with a book would restore my humour.

I sank into the oil-laden waters, letting the perfume lap at my hair, and closed my eyes. There was a knock at the door.

'Come in,' I called, taking care to fold my legs prettily to my stomach to avoid the maid's discomfiture. Nothing happened.

'It's Kit,' came the explanation. For a moment I didn't recognize his voice.

'Well? Come in,' I said with authority. This was getting interesting.

He appeared at the doorway. Hesitation didn't become him.

'I said, come in,' I repeated, patting the water's surface. 'I won't ask again.'

He removed his clothes with care, folding and laying each item to avoid crushing the cloth. I watched with approbation. It boded well.

I had chance to be introduced to each part of him at my leisure as his body was revealed. His shoulders were broad and well muscled. His arms were lean and sinewy. His chest was free of hair except for a fine line that gathered momentum at his navel and swept down in a hirsute path to his groin. He had very little buttock for my taste, but the hollow above the musculature of his thighs spoke of a stamina I looked forward to meeting. His organ was magnificent – even in repose.

I motioned for him to come and sit between my legs. It was not a large bath and as he lowered himself into the water I pulled myself up on to the roll-top edge behind him, all the better to caress his body.

I took the sponge and soap in hand and began to rub smooth circles on his skin. He dipped his head as the bath's vapours rose around us.

I used my hands to soap below the waterline, first his back, and then his chest. I then laid my cheek against his neck and slid my hands down across his taut stomach, following the trail to his genitals. They were already expecting the touch of my hands and I teased and stroked them as I passed them by, massaging his inner thigh, taking care to apply a slightly aggressive pressure of the fingertips in that region, but drawing back before I reached his penis.

I soaped my fingers again and brought my hands up his body to his nipples, encircling them slowly, feeling them harden beneath my palms.

I bade him stand up and as he turned around I had the pleasure to witness an erection of such standing that I was tempted to impale myself on it immediately – but that would have ruined the anticipation.

I steeled myself for my next line: 'To be resumed?' It was as much a statement as a question. I felt his body tense upon me and kissed his neck to lessen the blow. 'I must get dressed. They will soon be gathering for supper.'

I left him alone in the bathroom, and indeed he was still there forty minutes later when I descended the stairs for my next assignment, which simplified matters enormously when the maid returned to help me with my stays.

A liveried footman opened the door to the drawing room as I approached, and I turned sideways slightly to allow my dress to pass through. Everyone was present except for Mrs B and Kit. I recognized everyone except for the tall, Roman-nosed young woman who was sitting surrounded by the brace of stupidity that was Signor L and Miss B. They were fawning over her every word.

'Ah, here you are, my dear,' fussed Mr B. 'Come, let me introduce Mrs MacGregor.' It was the Scottish widow. I had been wrong to imagine her as an old crone. She was also extremely handsome. His Grace obviously thought so too. I was irritated by this intrusion into the game and I watched carefully throughout dinner for signs of a challenge to my position.

Unfortunately the Duke seemed to favour both of us and conversed politely with both his left and right during dinner. Such was my consternation that I invested precious little time in catching Kit's eye in order to secure a later rendezvous with him. Needs must.

During an interminable card game accompanied by the inevitable foot of Signor L, I was delighted to hear the widow make her apologies and retire. I thus relaxed into a well-practised formula that allowed me to hold the party's attention easily with a mixture of wit and gossip – something which has become part of my battery of weapons. At last the Duke found cause to reach down to the floor, picking up a fallen card. Whilst he was down there he stroked my ankle and let his hand travel up to my knee. He then made his excuses to the assembled party and took his leave. As he kissed my hand he lifted his eye to mine, his brow raised expectantly. I knew what he anticipated.

I returned to my room as soon as it was polite to do so and, with the aid of a maid, reduced my attire to a simple but voluminous nightgown. I bade her goodnight and made a good deal of blowing out the candle. Once she had gone I tiptoed to the door and, checking that the corridor was clear, hurried to the Duke's room. The door was left slightly ajar and I entered silently.

The Duke was waiting and, closing the door quickly behind me, set to in the greedy removal of my nightgown. I allowed him to paw at my neck and suck my breasts before he led me into the bedchamber.

I was not a little annoyed to find the widow already in his bed. She winked at me, which lessened my anger a little, but still I swore to get this over with as quickly as possible, and with the least effort on my part.

My rival pulled back the sheets, and the Duke led me to her. I turned and bid him join us too; I had not the heart for faux-Sapphic love this evening – it was late and the day had held enough obstacles to true pleasure already. The Duke launched at us and through deft and quick movements of my body I effected control of the sequence of movements. I ensured that the Duke penetrated her first and I licked them both as he entered her; I then encouraged him deftly to withdraw so that she too could pleasure him with her mouth.

We ended up quite comfortably. I sat propped up against the headboard, supported by a wealth of soft pillows, touching myself for the Duke's enjoyment while the widow lay on her back between my legs. In this way I could encourage the Duke to thrust his cock back and forth between her breasts whilst he licked mine, thus leaving her to her own devices where it came to arranging her own pleasure. None too soon, he ejected a stream of silver semen over her neck and chin. With that they both fell into a heavy sleep and I stroked them both, to ensure they were in deep repose, before I knew it would be safe to take my leave.

Back in my chamber, I was first deflated to find my bed untouched, then quickly heartened to realize that I had not received a visit from Mr B and his yearning buttocks. I had only had my eyes closed for a minute, however, when I heard the door open and close and I recognized the outline of my would-be lover. His thumb pressed my lips again and I bit it lightly between my teeth. We fell into each other's arms with an abandon that gave the lie to my earlier fatigue. And I can assure you that he was as proficient with his tongue as he was with his fingers and his cock, and at one point an inanimate object that he had procured from my bedside, which to this day I cannot remember except for the pleasure it wrought out of me through his expert hands.

The next morning I awoke to the relief that I could leave. Yes, I had had my fun, but it may have been that the Duke slept the whole night with the Scottish widow, and it might be conceived that I had lost the upper hand.

After breakfast we repaired to the little sitting room overlooking the garden for our coffee and chocolate. I settled next to the host, who took my hand reassuringly. A few pleasantries were exchanged – my departure was imminent – and I was just about to take my leave when the Duke came in carrying a small narrow velvet box.

'Forgive me, my dear, for taking the liberty, but last night after supper I could not help but notice that your beauty could only have been complemented by this small gift.' He opened the box before my eyes to reveal a triple string of pearls. The irony was not lost on me. I accepted gratefully, not least because it signified triumphant laurels. I noticed from the corner of my eye that Mr B was clasping his hands together and that the Scottish widow was leaving the room.

I said my goodbyes to everyone I could find and

returned to complete my packing. As I passed through the hallway to the stairs I glanced through a doorway left slightly ajar. Through it I could see an orchid room and, at the other side of the orchid table, I could just make out the euphoric stance of Signor L, head back, eyes firmly shut as he steadied himself against the wall. I looked for the cause of this elation and discerned the Scottish lady was down on her knees, pleasuring him with admirable ferocity. She glanced up and caught my eye defiantly. It was not a moment for jealousy. I raised the velvet jewel box in a gesture of farewell and swept along the corridor in triumph.

III

I AM YOUR MUSE

I let the wrap fall from my body for him. The air was cold and my skin felt hard and smooth, like marble. I was unveiling myself for him – a living sculpture. His hand stroked the curve of my back and came to rest on my behind. It was generously warm. My nipples, already as taut as granite, stiffened further.

'The cold,' he acknowledged. He stepped back, continuing his appraisal. Minutes passed. We both stood as still as stone. It was impossible to read his thoughts. With a prickle of unease, I realized I might not be what he needed. This notion was not one I often encounter. I had travelled for three days to get here; there had been trouble with a connection of the trains at Lyons. My cheeks reddened with consternation. Is my whole body blushing, I wondered? If it was, the blush deepened now, as I became angered by my position. I should leave, I decided, but he interrupted my thoughts.

'We must start.' His voice was firm but his attitude was one of detachment. 'We have lost a day. I will organize the stove later.' Cold comfort. He pulled up a high stool and rested against it. His eyes traversed my limbs.

I had learned a little about him from the friend who had recommended me to him. His name was César. He was a follower of the 'Realist' school. He worshipped Courbet. He was a great fuck.

It was July and the temperature outside was more than pleasant, but the studio light entered grey and pale from the north window. At this early hour of the morning the heat had not yet penetrated.

His attentive eye continued to brush around my body.

I glanced up at the balcony at the end of the room – I could just see the end of the bed which had been shown to me as mine. It lay above the studio amid sparse furnishings. I was to be here for over a month – I had expected more privacy. I am used to control – of all situations. It was only a minor setback, I reasoned; a whole summer of afternoons to myself in the French countryside lay ahead of me.

I wondered how soon it would be before we would sleep together. I looked back at him. He seemed oblivious to my gaze. That must be why my bed was in his studio, away from the main house, so he could follow his creative urges – at any time. The arrogance of the artist, I assumed. I like arrogance.

He was not markedly attractive but his physique was strong, quiet. He looked 'happy in his own skin' as they would say here. He seemed to harbour an air of brooding melancholy that made me want to explore him further.

'I cannot see you clearly. Your face reveals that you think always of sex.' The statement made me flinch. 'Don't posture.' I wondered how to respond. He was right, but this was not a valid criticism. How else can you allow a stranger access to your body?

'Look at me,' he demanded. 'No, not like that. Look towards me. Don't throw a "personality" at me. Present nothing with your mind. Simply reveal your body.' I could do this – but did I want to do it? I felt a strange sensation, a long-forgotten emotion: shyness.

'Oh, relax,' he said, looking me straight in the eye. 'Anyone can fuck. Not everyone can hold his or her body with pride, as God intended. Fucking is only part of that.'

His words were matter-of-fact, and for that no less shocking. Even the word fuck – which I have heard so often used in seduction – seemed so raw, so revealed, in his mouth.

'Where is your pride?' he continued. 'You are a woman. You are blessed with a beautiful body simply by being born a female. And you are set apart from the majority of women by your particular beauty and yet you hold yourself like a common whore. I don't wish to paint a chimera.'

At that moment his assistant entered the studio. 'This is Paul,' explained César. 'He is a talented young man but has a lot to learn about loftier ideals.' Paul raised his eyebrows in mock surprise behind his mentor's back. He was young and tall and I noticed his long, beautiful fingers that encircled the pitcher of wine and three glasses. He caught me looking and returned my gaze with an air of amused interest. The immediate appreciation of my sexuality was impossible to miss. Despite César's attempts to train me, I returned his look with an equal measure of desire.

I broke off my gaze as César approached me again. He was behind me now. He put both hands either side of my waist. 'Think about it.' He shook me by the hips abruptly. I could only think about fucking him, and when I banished those thoughts they were replaced swiftly by images of being fucked by the beautiful Paul. I would have to work on his requirements. It would be a challenge.

In the afternoon I walked down the long drive, between the plane trees, to the village. It was good to be in the warm air. There was a bar to the side of the main square and I took a table in the shade beside the front door.

A young girl came out immediately to greet me. She could not have been more than eighteen years old. She wore a simple long black skirt and a white blouse with a little crucifix at her neck. Her breasts were constrained by the fabric. Every part of her youthful figure begged to break out of its wrapping and she carried herself with confidence. She exuded sexuality but, from her demeanour, refused to acknowledge it. She returned with a tray of lemon juice, water, ice and sugar syrup. As she bent over the table, I looked at her cleavage, at the little crucifix, and her youthful flesh. It was beguiling. Then I realized she was waiting to be paid.

I sat and drank my *citron pressé*, reflecting on all the conflicting impulses I had encountered since my arrival. It is true, I thought; I have had more sex than many of my contemporaries. I had thought that was why I had been recommended, that I had the right 'constitution' for this work. Maybe it was. But here was a demand I was not used to. I was not to 'be' anyone – but myself.

I returned to the house to find César drinking with friends. Valentin and Davide stood up immediately to introduce themselves; I knew that each of them was undressing me with their eyes. Paul was there too and raised a languid hand. They had been drinking heavily.

The atmosphere was relaxed and rowdy, the room full of a happy passion.

'So, you're the new model.' Davide pulled up a chair for me. 'Has César sequestered you over there to have his wicked way with you? Paul says you are sleeping on the balcony.'

'It's to protect her from you!' contested César. 'She hasn't come here for an orgy. She is my model. I am planning a work like the Master's *The Artist's Studio*.' Paul, hiccoughing slightly, pushed over a small reproduction of a painting for me to consider. It showed an artist at the easel with a nude model standing behind him surveying his work. All around them were various friends and admirers in local dress. 'I need a nude to represent the artist's inspiration. I want the truth, *la veritée*, not an idealized falsehood. I seek a monumental, heroic reality in which all are equal.' He spoke with passion but his friends just shook their heads and laughed.

'I will show you this artist's inspiration,' challenged Davide. 'This, too, is from the same brush!' He flicked the pages to where the book fell open easily to reveal a detailed painting of a woman's pudenda. It was startlingly graphic, unlike the smooth classical nudes I was used to seeing – here was pubic hair, parted labia and you could sense, despite this being only a detail of part of her body, the woman who owned this organ.

It was a woman who had either just been fucked or was about to be, she was either post-coital or expectant of such.

'*Voila*! *L'Origine du Monde*, the origin of the world!' proclaimed Davide. 'Here is the true origin of his motive and thus he has you sleeping in his studio. This is the view of a "real" woman he is searching for!'

César hit out at him but smiled resignedly. The men all laughed again and apologized for my embarrassment, though I had none – I was fascinated. Was I going to be painted like this? There certainly had been no sign yet of the 'great fuck' recommended by my friend.

'Oh, for God's sake,' railed César, obviously used to this line of argument. And then, revealing for the first time in our acquaintance a shred of empathy, he added in a low voice, 'I am insomniac – I rarely sleep at all when I am in the middle of a painting. Thus, if you sleep in the studio we can work at any time.' Then he kicked out at Davide's chair with mock aggression. 'And, of course, it will keep you apart from these wolves!'

The room descended into laughter again. We ate and drank late into the evening. Their company was relaxed and sympathetic. I liked their open licentiousness – compared to the intensity of César, it was a welcome relief. I surveyed each man in turn.

Paul was young and virile, relaxed in his own body – very flirty. Davide was slightly older and more stocky and all his movements spoke of a strength and firm purpose. Valentin looked kind and gentle, with a tall but slight body. His elfin face looked like that of a schoolteacher or young professor.

Paul caught my eye and raised his glass. Yes, I decided, it would be Paul with whom I would first sleep.

At midnight, sensing there was no end in sight to the evening, I made my apologies and left for the studio. My balcony sleeping space was quiet and the words and images conjured up by the raucous conversations flew around my head. I closed my eyes but all I could see was the painting of that woman's pussy. It was intoxicating to think about it; I investigated my own genitals with a lazy finger. I stroked the labia and wondered whether the painter had got the model to masturbate for him. I imagined doing that for César as I touched myself, but I couldn't hold the picture of his face in my mind and before long it was that of Paul which took his place. I brought myself to a shuddering climax and fell asleep. My dreams were filled with thoughts of me lying prone in the studio for César whilst Paul, Davide and Valentin took turns to worship at the altar of my pussy. David was the most analytical – he parted my labia and licked and tasted me, using his tongue to push up inside me to see how wet I was becoming. He seemed to approve and recommended me heartily to Valentin as 'a real woman', not a sculpture. Valentin then took his place – we smiled at each other reassuringly – and as he blew gently at my pudenda, to open my legs further, he reached up with his long arms to stroke my breasts and stomach, coaxing multiple sonorous orgasms from me as he licked and nibbled and sucked at me. Paul, I noticed, sat watching the images of my sex that César created on the canvas.

I was woken early by the sounds of César and Paul as they moved below me in the studio. Paul had lit the stove and the smell of coffee soon pervaded the space. After we had breakfasted Paul cleared the little table of bread and jam and returned to the farmhouse with the remains. César and I began our work and he sketched furiously with renewed vigour.

A little later Paul came in and sat by César, by turns watching him sketch with a respectful eye and then looking at me with a very different appraisal. Despite my best efforts, he would catch my eye with an expression that was all suggestion. I smiled slightly.

César threw down his sketchbook violently. 'For the love of Christ, can't you give it a rest, you two? I have told you what I am trying to achieve. I am a professional voyeur, Paul. I can only embrace life through the eye. I cannot feel reality until I have captured it on my canvas. That is Art, Paul. Capturing a pretty girl's eye so you can fuck her is not Art, it's an animal urge. It's not wrong, but it is easy. It is not what I am striving for here.'

Paul held his hands up, chuckling guiltily. I shifted the cotton drape a little closer around me.

'If you can't take it seriously then you had better leave.'

'OK! OK! I am going.' Paul retreated from the scene, incriminating himself by revealing César's analysis to be true. I felt secretly pleased and then sensed an immediate flush of warmth between my legs.

César brought me back sharply. 'And you . . . you are beautiful and free to embrace life with your body, but you don't yet know how to rise above the male gaze. Accept it as a compliment, of course, but you don't have to return it in kind. Learn that skill and you will hold every man in thrall.' I saw his vehement expression and I looked directly into his eyes. I realized that it was one of the first times I had held a man's passionate look whilst being entirely detached from any sexual overtone. It felt empowering. I also felt liberated.

'Now! There's the look I want!' shouted César

triumphantly. 'Remember how it feels. Stay like that.' I smiled with pride and relaxed into the morning session with a renewed sense of purpose.

After the session, I decided to take a walk. At the bottom of the hill I followed the path of the river until it came to a bend, where it widened into a deep pond sheltered by overhanging trees. The heat of the sun still permeated the afternoon and I decided to bathe.

As I took off my hat and folded up my long dress, searching for a dry rock on which to put them, I became aware of the muted sounds of moaning. I glanced around to see if I could trace the source of the noise. In the distance, beyond the rocks, in the shade of a large plane tree was the unexpected vision of Paul and the girl from the village bar. They were locked in an ecstatic embrace. She leaned against a tree and Paul was on his knees before her, his mouth working strenuously and masterfully at her pussy. Both were completely naked, and the beauty of her young body, so obvious yesterday despite her clothes, was fully revealed now. Her breasts were large and firm and they rose and fell with her moans as she thrust her pelvis again and again towards Paul's ravenous face. She had no inhibitions; her noise rose with her climax and her face was one of pure beauty in her ecstasy.

I felt rooted to the spot, privileged to see such open lovemaking. She let her hips fall back against the tree and grabbed at Paul's hair with both hands, then took a deep breath and let the air stream out through pursed lips. She laughed freely and knelt down in front of Paul, kissing him hungrily.

Paul took both sides of her heaving chest and turned her over on to all fours, spreading her knees apart with his own, and impaled her with such an expression of joy that I felt myself bite my bottom lip. The girl braced herself beneath his onslaught, commanding him on with loud entreaties. Her breasts swung and shook with the fervour of every movement. I wished that I too could feel the smooth soft flesh of her plump thighs between my fingers as Paul did now, pulling her backwards rhythmically as he shafted deep inside her. Her eyes were closed as tightly as her fists and I could see she was close to climaxing again. I too felt an intense and mounting pleasure.

I switched my gaze to Paul's wide smile – he was looking straight at me as he drove himself home. My insides immediately tensed at being caught peeping, but the deep pulsing between my own legs deepened. Paul nodded then closed his eyes and fell back into his own rapture. I twisted away, hesitant of my guilt. But Paul's look had been so complicit, so proud, that

I realized he was pleased to have been watched.

It was hard to get the image out of my mind and I could still see their coupling as I dived into the cool black waters of the pool. I could still feel the heat of the moment in my body and I luxuriated in the tiny currents and bubbles that licked around me as I swam beneath the surface. As the water slipped across my limbs, I fantasized that it was Paul's hands stroking me and then, enjoying the sensations this thought brought on, I imagined that both the girl and Paul swam with me, caressing and licking me. I pulled myself on to a submerged rock and, first checking for prying eyes, I stroked my nipples and encircled my clitoris so my body could shake off the stimulus that my own voyeurism had brought upon me.

That night I dreamed that, as a punishment, César posed us all, Davide, Valentin, Paul, the girl and I, in some fantastic orgiastic tableau: all limbs, tongues and mouths, which, he told us, was the lamentable *verité* of our minds.

The next morning, when I posed for César, I looked forward eagerly to Paul's arrival. Noting my disappointment, César revealed that he had banned him from attending our sessions, as it would distract me. It was true, of course. And it did make my lessons easier to learn without distraction. I had begun to enjoy my bond with this sullen artist. The sessions were liberating, and without distraction I began to discover the power of female beauty beyond that of sexual allure.

After lunch I strolled down into town to run a few errands. As I crossed the market square, I noticed the girl serving a customer in the bar. I caught her eye, but she showed no recognition. I decided not to stay for a drink and returned to the house. But when I reached the gravelled courtyard I was possessed by a different intention and carried on past the studio and garden to the meadow beyond and then on, down the hill, to the river. The heat of the day had not waned and my body was hot and sticky after such a long walk. I longed to cool it in the water.

The pool felt less chilly than the day before and I swam for a long time before my body felt uncomfortable. I pulled myself out onto a sunny rock to catch the last warm rays of the day and fell into a happy reverie. I wondered how much this experience would change me on my return to London.

I stretched out and closed my eyes, feeling completely at ease. The cicadas sang busily all around me and small flies alighted momentarily on my warm skin until I flicked them away with a lazy hand. I became aware of one particularly annoying insect that kept returning to my navel. I brushed it away again and again until I had a moment's respite. Then it found my nipple and repeated its habit. When it moved to tickle my pubis I took exception and opened my eyes to investigate. To my consternation I saw not a small fly, but the end of a long stalk of flowering grass. My tormentor was Paul, who lay on his side gently teasing me.

He smiled the same broad smile that had come to act as a key to the space between my legs. I smiled back and he reached out to stroke my cheek with the grass. He traced its passage slowly down my face, and continued the motion down my neck, then drew broad figures of eight around my breasts. We locked eyes quickly – his were bluer than I had realized. His appetite matched mine; there was an instant physical understanding. He threw the grass away and pulled himself closer to me, bringing his face down above mine until our lips almost touched. I could feel his breath on my nose and mouth. His eyes still bore into mine and I felt his hand reach down my inner thigh.

We stayed like that for several moments as my breathing became more and more exaggerated. His hand moved almost imperceptibly towards its goal and I pushed my hips forwards impatiently. At last I felt his fingers touch my sex. He toyed at the entrance, pushing and retracting only the tips of his finger teasingly between my folds. I began to moan softly. It was sweet agony. I longed for him to fill me. Slowly, he slid a finger deep inside; then, to a sigh of protest, he withdrew. He lifted his finger to his mouth and sucked it provocatively. At last, his mouth covered mine and I tasted myself on his tongue as he drove three long fingers inside me. They quested over and over with the same rhythm. I arched my back and pressed against him. Then he was inside me, his hand tightening upon my breast as we pushed ourselves together without mercy.

And thus the summer continued. My days and nights were split into two distinct activities. I would pose for César every morning and often, as his drive to finish his painting grew more voracious and his insomnia increased, he would wake me during the night when he couldn't sleep. I became used to his needs and even dependent upon his respectful inquisitive gaze, which I found I could now return in equal measure. In the afternoons I would meet Paul and we would share one another's bodies. It was a happy arrangement.

When César moved from sketches to the canvas he needed me less and less and I found myself meeting more infrequently with Paul – it was as if my baser appetites abated as the painting came closer and closer to completion.

At last the day came for me to leave. I had begged and begged César to show me the painting, but to no avail. I took one last look at the simple bed and table that had been my bolthole for the summer and carried my bag down the iron steps.

César was waiting for me at the easel. 'Do you want to see what you can be?' he asked.

My heart bumped against the wall of my chest. 'Yes, of course,' I said eagerly.

He turned the canvas around to me and I gazed upon a portrayal of myself I had never seen before.

I was depicted at the centre of the canvas as the Artist, my nude body only partially obscured by a large canvas upon which I was painting. I held a palette in my left hand and a brush in my right. My gaze was directed straight ahead into the viewer's eyes, as if the whole world was my subject. My body was depicted as beautiful but real. The soft brown curls of my pubic hair were realized without uniformity, the slight puckering of the flesh of my thighs minutely rendered. My expression was one of strength and confidence.

The message of the piece seemed clear to read. One dared not look at my nakedness with anything close to sensual hunger – even though my lack of clothes was emphasized in the eye of the viewer by the fact that the figure in the chair to the right of my canvas was fully dressed. It was, I realized, a depiction of Paul, sitting unusually still. His interested gaze was directed not at me but at the canvas, his face portraying study without lasciviousness.

I felt humbled by the emotion infused in this scene. I reached out and put my hand gently on César's shoulder. I was just about to try and speak when my eye alighted on the mirror at the back of the scene. There, minutely rendered in the reflection, was the image of César in supine repose, sleeping deeply. Free at last of the insomnia that plagued him during his quest to 'embrace life' in the canvas. Did this denote that this was only, could only be, the dream of the artist? I felt it was something I would ponder for years to come.

I was unable to find the appropriate words, so I just squeezed his shoulder and brushed a kiss on his cheek. Tears sprang to my eyes and César laughed loudly. Then, with a resounding slap, he smacked at my bottom, bringing me to my senses. 'And for my naughty girl, something to remember us all by. Hide it well in your packing. The port authorities might take exception.'

He winked as he handed me a small, rolled-up canvas. I pulled it open slowly and my eyes widened at the scene revealed to me. There, depicted on the raised dais of the artist's studio, was a monumental display of wanton flesh and passion. The four naked revellers depicted were statuesque figures, almost warlike in their poses, and yet their actions were not those normally played out in public. Two men and a girl disported themselves together, she on all fours hungrily taking the shaft of the man in front of her into her mouth. Her beautiful creamy buttocks were being lifted by the two strong arms of the man behind her as he pulled her body on to his astonishingly large shaft. Their faces were transfixed with ecstasy. In a chair to the right of the canvas sat another man lost in private reverie, legs wide apart, pleasuring himself as he surveyed the scene. The figures on the dais were unmistakably Davide, Valentin and the girl from the bar. Paul, of course, was the easy voyeur in the chair. And again, there in the mirror at the back of the composition was the reflection of the artist himself, sleeping deeply. This time, however, he held another sleeping figure in his arms, loosely covered in a drape that obscured her breasts and buttocks. It was me.

I lowered myself carefully down on my heels in front of the man of whom I knew so little and looked into his eyes. He smiled. I pressed a deep, dry, full-lipped kiss on to his mouth, and took my leave.

IV

I AM YOUR PRIVATE DANCER

I dance occasionally at a revue bar in the less salubrious part of the city. The decadence of the nightlife crowds are a marked relief from the monotony and disillusion of modern life.

Tonight I had danced alone, on a chair – a cliché, but it works.

I have, as they say, 'what it takes'. I am supple. My thighs are strong. The face doesn't matter – make-up can cope with that – but you need a terrific body, curves in all the right places. (A wraith's body just won't hook them.) These attributes alone will get you through, but combine them with a command of timing and a mastery of anticipation and you will have your audience baying for you. And when you dance, every move, however 'innocent', must throw up pictures of sex in their mind's eye. As you hunker down on your heels they must feel you grinding in their lap.

It is an act. You are their apparition. You must transport them to the darkest recesses of their yearnings.

I have the skill to do this.

The door opened and we flooded out into the dark of the side street, each girl suddenly sobered by their sombre winter coats. Some still wore the vestiges of strong make-up around their eyes or had their hair pulled back. Goodnights rang out in either direction as we went our separate ways. Some arm in arm, to party, some to meet a lover, others, like me, to get an 'early' night. It was two in the morning. If I walked quickly, I could be home in ten minutes.

I felt the wall against my right cheek before I felt the hand that pushed me there. It now insinuated itself into my hair and refused to let me turn. The bricks were wet and gritty. The cold seeped into the corner of my mouth. A tall, strong body crushed against mine. I had only managed to free one hand, its fingers splayed into the greasy chill of the wall. It was useless to push. My other hand was a prisoner, deep in the pocket that refused to free it.

'Hello,' whispered the voice in my ear. 'Leaving...' The whisper trailed off into a treacherous giggle.

I could smell the alcohol. He tried again. Found a better tenor. 'Leaving without . . .' the voice suddenly calmed into insidiousness. 'Without so much as a . . .

by' – his hips thrust harder against me – 'your' – thrust again – 'leave?' He growled, thrust again and kept up the pressure. The pain of my hip pushed into my wrist, even through the layers of wool, was excruciating.

The hand in my hair began to relax its grip. It now slowly caressed the nape of my neck. I became aware first of my breathing and then of his. There was no reciprocity to the rhythm: our bodies seemed to batter against each other although the distance between us was infinitesimal. The stroking fingers were no relief. Then they began to twist and probe and twist again, tighter and tighter. My pulse quickened. I had no idea what was going to happen. The hand was firmly enmeshed in my damp curls now, the hot palm against my scalp. Its warmth was a hypocritical comfort.

Suddenly, I was whirled around, pulled close into his neck; his hand still cradled my matted hair whilst his left arm thrust itself round me. Lost in the maze of collars and cloth, the curls of hair escaping from the top of his shirt pricked my nose. We stayed like this for some seconds and then I began to feel his body shake. At first it was a shudder, then came a larger more uncontrolled spasm. I struggled to free myself, but despite his loss of composure I won only an inch of freedom. Finally his laughter broke free, erupting in waves, and I could look up into his face.

He was an Adonis with a sweep of dirty blond hair. He relaxed his grip and fell into me. The night was pierced by his high-pitched boyish giggles. He had a body built for war but it housed the mind of a child. I was only mildly relieved to recognize him. I brought my hand to his cheek with as much force as I could muster. He accepted the pain almost gratefully and attempted to plant a conciliatory kiss on the bridge of my nose. I ducked out of the way and turned to face him.

'I wasn't expecting you,' I said as patiently as I could.

'We said Friday,' he asserted, sobering suddenly. We hadn't, but it didn't pay to argue.

'You said you want to see me dance with Amber?'

'I do.'

'Well, that's tomorrow –'

'I watched you tonight,' he blurted. There was pain in his words. They broke in over mine. I was extremely tired. But I knew this mood: childish, needy, selfish. He wouldn't leave until he had got what he wanted.

I didn't have the energy to stay up all night trying to postpone the moment. Nor would I take him home. He had never been to my flat, and I wanted it to stay that way. I was very fond of him, as one would be of an overgrown puppy, but he was dangerous. It was then that I realized with surprise that the flood of relief, crashing with adrenaline, now spawned a reckless desire. If there was one thing I had come to love about him it was his spontaneity. Perhaps that is why I saw him again and again when most other women would have tired of his infantile ego. But the spontaneity was infectious. And I had caught it.

His power was immense; he pushed me back against the wall with ease. He lifted enormous hands to my shoulders to steady himself while I unbuckled his belt. He looked into my eyes. I could see how hard it was for him to focus. He suddenly looked chastened. He would have to concentrate now or let himself down.

'Did you enjoy watching me?' I tested him. For an answer, I slid my hand down to his genitals. They were pulsating but far from hard. I could profit from this.

'You can't do it, can you?' I snarled. His cock seemed to flinch. His hand flew to his trousers. His anger was growing. His cock, his face, his whole body seemed to grow in size in front of me.

'Can't I?' He seemed suddenly out of breath. Reaching down with one arm, he hooked me behind the thighs, dragging my whole body up off the floor, up against him. I wrapped my left leg around him, he hoisted up the other. My back bumped against the wall and I was glad of my thick coat. When he wrenched the crotch of my pants aside I realized how very wet I was. I sank down on him and he bucked inside me.

'What am I doing now?' His eyes were all filmy. He demanded again, 'What am I doing?'

'Fucking me,' I confided softly, repeatedly, allowing him to hear the break in my voice. And so we continued over and over until he began to make a strange wailing noise. I noticed someone turn to walk down our street, but they were repelled by the violent coupling they witnessed.

'Someone's watching us,' I warned, knowing exactly what his response to this stimulus would be, loving the control. His balls tightened; his shaft engorged. I gripped him with all my might and shivered down on to him with release. I hadn't intended to come. His wail increased to a long, pained monotone and he thrust his mouth over mine. I seemed to swallow his noise too. I pulled away, gasping for air. All was still and silent.

He raised his brows; the giggles were starting again. I slipped back down to my feet and pulled my coat tightly around me, knotting the belt. I stepped away. It was time to leave.

Tears streamed down his cheeks. He was battling to say something. He threw his head back and, between the laughter, began to crow. I turned away.

'Go home, Marcus.'

I left him leaning against the wall, trousers around his ankles, chortling triumphantly. It was hard not to admire his devastating exhibitionism.

Infrequently I am called in to dance with Amber. Sometimes it is at the whim of the club's manager, but mostly it is Amber's suggestion. Amber is their star. She is infamously, rapaciously lesbian. She is also the most mesmerizing performer, with a voice like gravel and honey. I have known and loved her since we met at theatre school.

When I am called in, I like to arrive early, to get my make-up on and my costume (always stockings, suspenders and a basque – the manager insists that it is the base to all our costumes) with enough time to move among the chorus girls, chatting and smoking with them. Or I curl up on the velvet cushions of Amber's window seat and laugh at the world's follies until it is time for her to go on.

The corridor that leads to the dressing room is, like the rest of the club, decorated with vestiges of the Weimar Republic. This imbues the nights with an air of decadence, but seems pathetic and tawdry in the daylight that occasionally manages to penetrate the building.

I entered Amber's dressing room. Her costumes, too, hang limply in the day, revealing their stitches and broken sequins. But at night this becomes a fetishist's treasure chest.

I sat and watched her happily this evening as she applied her lipstick. She smacked her lips and pushed herself round on her chair to face me. 'Ta-da!' she said theatrically. I laughed.

'All yours, my dear,' she said, motioning to the chair. 'When is your friend arriving?'

I groaned and walked over to the dressing table. I knelt on the chair to face the mirror and picked up the brush to pull back my hair. There was a knock at the door. I jumped unnecessarily. 'Two minutes, Miss D,' came the muffled voice of the caller.

'He asked if he could meet you after the show,' I confessed. Amber stalked to the mannequin that stood impotent and heavily laden between us and the door. She removed a ludicrously large and feathered head-dress. She was an Amazon.

'I'm looking forward to it!' she promised, and with a shake of her tail feather to my mirrored reflection she flounced out of the door.

The door slammed immediately again. 'Forgotten something?' I called out. I heard the bolt being drawn across and looked up.

'You could say that.'

It was Marcus. His timing was always immaculately inappropriate. But it wouldn't do to show my frustration. Anyway, it was impossible not to appreciate his beauty. I smiled. The sense of danger that accompanied him made me desire him more. He approached and pulled the chiffon robe off my shoulder. He scratched my neck, then licked it. Pleasure and pain.

But now was not the time. I had ten minutes maximum to get ready and this could get messy. I thought quickly.

'Amber is looking forward to meeting you later, you know,' I said casually. He begged and panted like a dog, and yelped eagerly. This strategy could work – I just had to keep calm, keep control of the situation. 'Let me get ready now.' He didn't move.

'I need to get ready,' I implored, and changed tactic, playing to his vanity. 'You distract me too much.'

It backfired. His brows knitted. 'Are you trying to get rid of me?' He reached past me, picked up an orange from the bowl on the dressing table and began to toss it and catch it repeatedly while staring at me. I felt the menace of the moment. 'Come on, baby, just give me a minute.'

I affected nonchalance but my heart was racing as I applied my false eyelashes. I knew Marcus was capable of violent switches of mood, especially if thwarted.

The orange fell again and again into his ample palm. Slap. Slap. Slap.

'Well? Are you?'

Slap . . . Slap . . . Slap. The intervals were wider now as he threw it higher each time. I chanced a look at him. He was staring straight at me. Not even looking at the orange that he caught each time with monotonous and unswerving precision. A chill moved through me – if I had not been so anxious that this diversion would make me miss my cue I would have been inexorably turned on. I allowed myself to melt a little at the thought and immediately felt signs of longing between my legs. He caught the look and immediately stilled the orange ball. And smiled.

'Ah, there it is.' Please, not now, I thought, not now. If only the knock on the door would come.

His lips brushed the skin of my shoulder. 'Please, Marcus . . .' The panic rose in my voice and he fed off it. He ripped the gown from my shoulders like a bull-fighter whips his cape. My arms were bared but the long row of buttons at the satin cuffs would not pass my hands. He forced my arms backwards and the chiffon sleeves became a pair of reins. Marcus was visibly delighted. He pulled them in tight and bundled them into one capacious hand. He grabbed a fistful of hair and yanked.

I could just make out my reflection; it was the image of subjection. I felt both fear and excitement.

Marcus passed the body of the gown over his head

and around his shoulders, harnessing himself to me. I was powerless. He pushed me forwards so that my chest rested on the back of the chair, then my stomach fell as he rocked the chair on to its back legs, leaning precariously against the surface of the dressing table.

Laying his arms over my shoulder, he began to knead and press the flesh of the orange in front of my face with both hands. The fruit was brought closer still to my nose. He ran his nail across the peel. A cloud of essence rose into my eyes. I breathed it in, could taste it at the back of my throat. It made my eyes sting, but I knew better than to complain. I returned his gaze in the mirror, as equally as I could muster. I must not threaten this dangerous child. He dragged his nail across the fruit again and then suddenly impaled it with his thumb. I could feel his excitement hardening him. There was no going back. The only rescue would be to get this over with as quickly as possible. I smiled and pushed back against him.

'Ahh, little Pleasure! You are here!' he exclaimed with joy, leaning back from me slightly. He threw up his hands in delight and I tried, without effect, to change my position. He deftly peeled the orange and then broke it in half, holding both halves easily in one palm. He bit and sucked at it nonchalantly then, without warning, ripped away my satin underwear.

'No!' I exclaimed hotly. Not my costume. He had

longed for that. He wanted me angry. I fought against my shackles. In spite of myself, I was feeling the swell of desire.

The gown shifted and I could move my hands to the side of my thighs. I threw my weight back to sit up. But he was a Goliath of a man and adjusted the chair, even with me on it, with ease. I found myself thrown forwards even more, my buttocks raised to him.

He steadied himself on my hips – my arms were now pinned firmly, horizontally, against my sides. He surveyed the curve of my body and turned his head on its side to look at my arsehole and pussy. He puckered hard and blew gently. As the current of air hit my parted labia I realized how hot I had become. Damn him.

I protested again.

'What's wrong, little Pleasure?' he purred. 'What do you want?' He searched for desire in my eyes. I tried to keep it hidden.

'Oh, how selfish of me!' he suddenly exclaimed and, like a conjuror, he produced the uneaten half of the orange in the tips of his fingers, flourishing it to an invisible audience in the mirror. Then, with a nod that I should pay attention, he swung his arm back behind my body. I felt him palm the orange against the flesh of my sex, pressing the melting fruit into my clitoris, slipping it backwards and forwards until it was entirely gloved by my labia. The juice rose up and fell again in the entrance to my vagina. It was impossible to resist. I gasped.

'That's it, my Pleasure. You can't stop me, can you? Tell me to stop!' he demanded. I tried to answer, but the words seemed stuck in my throat.

'What's that little one?' he coaxed. 'Come on, stop me!' His smile was broad and victorious. He stroked my breasts with his right hand and forearm, caressing my nipples. The flesh of the fruit slid rhythmically within its pocket. I was unbearably close.

His finger moved to my clitoris and made sharp burning little circles. I felt myself move back from the brink. I opened my eyes. He abandoned my breasts for his buckle and deftly undid his trousers to expose himself. His cock was extremely large and handsome. He stroked himself for a while. He was preening.

I watched, mesmerized. Then his eyes lighted on the open pot of cold cream. He stopped pleasuring himself and pressed his thumb into the white unguent.

He let up with the orange slightly and pressed it half up inside me. I gasped. Then I felt the flat of his thumb at my anus. Slowly he began trace a circle around it, pressing first with firm pressure, then with soft. His teasing became unbearable. My first climax was inexorable. I moaned. I could feel the juice of the orange begin to run down my inner thigh.

'That's my Pleasure,' he coaxed. My sense of what was Marcus and what was the fruit was becoming confused. The juices ran between my legs. He spread the cream back and forth across my backside, spreading the grease in smooth, widening circles over my buttocks. I fought against the tide that rose again, but the more I tried to deny it the stronger it built inside me.

'You can't stop me,' he whispered, removing the fruit. I tasted its juice on his left hand as he tried to push it into my mouth. I parted my teeth slightly and bit down on his thumb hard as I rose to a stupendous orgasm.

His cry of pain was almost jubilant and I felt my arms yanked back again. He thrust the whole length of his penis inside me and fucked and fucked my shaking body as the angle of the chair allowed him to plumb the very depths of me. His thumb pressed further and further inside me. I abandoned all rational thought; we were both lost in a wild race to the finish.

Marcus bucked and reared behind me, pulling me back harder and harder on to him. He stiffened and ground to a halt. His eyes rolled up into his skull. There was a sharp knock at the door. 'Two minutes to curtain!' called a voice. I began to shake violently and felt him, as if in slow motion, explode inside me. The buttons on one sleeve finally gave way. I was released. Marcus staggered backwards, breaking his fall on a pile of discarded costumes.

I pushed the chair upright with numb arms and slumped down on my heels, steeling myself. I had no time to lose. I sat up again, yanked off the remaining sleeve and threw it over Marcus's exposure. I was spent but exhilarated. I dragged back my hair and thrust the bobbed wig down over my crown. The transformation was instantaneous. I wiped myself proficiently with a towel and threw it at Marcus's face. He laughed and caught it, held it to his face and inhaled loudly.

'Clean yourself up,' I demanded.

'Yes, Mummy,' he wheedled. I scooped up the ripped knickers and threw them in the bin.

There was a bang at the door, the lock gave way and there was Amber looking a little surprised. I could hear the applause flooding in behind her. She stopped in the centre of the room, flushed with her own success.

'You're on,' she said, then noticed my lack of underwear.

She lifted an eyebrow. I gestured to the floor.

She quizzed me silently with no judgement, then in a swift move she removed her own knickers and handed them to me. I stepped into them. They were warm and slightly damp – not unpleasantly so.

Marcus applauded. Amber smiled patronizingly at him and moved to the dressing table.

She winked at me. 'We'll be fine, darling. Your guest can help me change. I will be out there in two minutes.' Marcus looked like the cat that had got the cream. I strapped on my gladiator's breastplate, put on the plumed helmet, grabbed the sword and ran out of the door.

The premise of this particular act is simple. I play a gladiator. To warm up I have to kill some slaves – played winsomely by the girls of the chorus. Then, to an ominous drum roll, enter Amber, stage left. She is the beautiful wild panther, whom I have to fight, then kill. It's a very camp piece, but the audience seem to lap it up.

Marcus certainly did. As Amber writhed around me on the small stage that separated us from the tables of the audience and I finally impaled her with my sword, I could see from the expression on his face that he was all anticipation.

Amber and I fell back through the dressing-room door laughing riotously, throwing off the ridiculous costumes. I felt invincible in her presence. I stopped to gather myself. Perhaps together we could remain unassailable. The door burst open. Right on cue, I thought.

Marcus stumbled in carrying three bottles of

champagne and three glasses. He was wearing the jacket of an SS uniform that he had obviously found lying around backstage. Amber stopped laughing. 'You'll take that off in here,' she said slowly.

I sensed danger in the air. 'Come on, let's drink!' I urged, grabbing the glasses. Marcus stayed where he was. I was unsure how he would react to Amber's orders. I wrenched a bottle from him and poured a glass. I turned to look at Amber.

She stood defiantly, hand on hip. Without averting her gaze, she reached out and took a glass from me and drained it. She motioned for another. She drained that. A smile crept on to Marcus's mouth. He held his hand out for a glass.

'No,' said Amber. 'Remove the jacket.'

'. . . Or?'

'Or . . . you won't see any of this.' She wrapped her arm around me and pulled me close to her, then kissed me proprietarily. With relief I saw Marcus begin to slide the jacket off his shoulders. Then Amber lifted her long booted leg, rested it upon his chest, and pushed. Her judgement was perfect – he was totally drunk. He fell back on to the chair at the dressing table.

'Give him a glass,' she relented with a sigh. His head lolled slightly and his pale blue eyes seemed to lose more of their colour. 'We're going to shower,'

Amber informed him. She winked at me. She was having fun.

Marcus grabbed a bottle and poured himself another glass. He was settling in for the show. Amber gently manoeuvred me until I stood astride his legs and we began our performance.

She peeled away each layer of my clothing. She was dancing for him. First she dipped down my body and released my stockings from the suspenders. She followed them down with her tongue. Then she worked her way up again to my inside thigh. Transfixed, Marcus fumbled slowly with his flies. She removed my underwear and squatted behind me, thrusting her hand up through my legs to cover my pubic hair with her flattened palm. She peeked out at Marcus from behind my legs – first one side and then the other. She then pointed aloft with her index finger and, rising slowly behind me on her stiletto heels, she dragged her finger down over my pubis, over my clitoris, through my folds, over my perineum and up between my buttocks. She was standing tall now, undoing my corset.

Marcus was standing erect. He looked so absurdly happy. I wanted to assemble myself on him, taking advantage of his unusually docile mood, but I let Amber choreograph our assault on him. My body rocked backwards as she unfastened the long row of hooks at my back and freed my upper body.

My breasts swung free. Amber cupped them both and kissed my neck. Marcus reached forwards but Amber tutted. He held up both hands to protest his innocence, unaware that he still held the glass and bottle. Champagne splashed on my body. Amber licked it off. The ache between my legs began to throb. I tried to work out whom I wanted the most.

Amber smacked my bottom. 'Go and shower, while I dance for him. Leave the door open.'

I watched them as the warm jets of water ran over the back of my neck. I soaped my breasts in a slow circular motion, savouring the thought of what would happen. Amber slowly stripped in front of him, but I knew she was doing it for me. My breasts were swollen; the nipples felt as hard as they had ever been. One after another her clothes were thrown at Marcus. He began to slip further and further down the chair.

She poured him more champagne and stepped behind him, stroking his hair. He began to sing, then stood up, demanding my presence. Amber aimed her boot again and he stumbled and fell heavily into the pile of clothes and cushions on the floor. He tried without success to get up, then slumped face down, insensible.

'My turn, darling,' said Amber. 'Leave the water running, will you?' As she passed me she kissed me fully on the lips and laughed. I wrapped myself in the towel and fell back on the long velvet cushions of her windowsill, exhausted. One nervous look at Marcus reassured me that he was out cold.

I was tired, but still felt the need for relief, so lifted my right leg and stroked myself reassuringly, thinking of Amber's body, admiring her control. I was nearly asleep when Amber joined me. She had turned the lights out.

'Move over, my love.' She shoved me playfully.

I groaned. She protested and swung her left leg over mine, then lifted my right thigh and used my hips to slide her leg under it and pull me to her, pubis to pubis. I was too tired to put up any resistance. Nor did I want to. She lay back on the window seat. The lips of our sex touched like a kiss and she twisted herself closer in to me.

We stayed like that for hours. Moving slowly, monotonously. Sweet, slow orgasms passed backwards and forwards between us in endless waves, like a deep slow burn.

V

I AM A CHILD OF THE SIXTIES

My friend Peter invited me to my first swinging party (although I don't think I knew it as that at the time). Peter had a sex drive equal to mine and a level of curiosity which knocked mine into a cocked hat.

We had been lovers at university. We had little in common in terms of lifestyle choices or background: he was more of an Essex boy with a penchant for seductions in Whitney-fuck-me-Houston surround-sound; I preferred a lost weekend in the soft grip of a natural chemical high and one of the new members of my ever-widening Bohemian circle. He called me his Child of the Sixties.

It was an affair that was passionate on a visceral level and almost telepathic on a platonic one. There was nothing in between – which meant that sex was exquisite and mind-blowing, but eventually we found ourselves more often laughing together in the bar than in bed. The fucking dried up; we became 'good friends'. The sex remains, however, some of the most fabulous I have ever had. He taught me much of what I practise today.

We bumped into each other through work some years later. I was as surprised as he was. It was in a faceless London hotel. Both of us wore a suit: mine accentuated what I hoped was the female power player I had become; his displayed the ruffled quality that comes with three days of business in town. It was only a brief encounter, but rewarding, not least because it earned me the invitation that was to broaden my horizons.

I must have been in my early twenties – far too young to realize that I was still young. Too naïve to suss out the true meaning of the scribble at the bottom of the invitation – 'bring a "plant", Sixties Child'. I took a poinsettia – it was just before Christmas and I judged the request must be for a house-proud wife. If I had loosened up and thought about the inverted commas, and the girl he might have remembered me as, I would have been better prepared for the atmosphere I would encounter.

I turned up on my own, fashionably late. I hadn't expected the electric gates, the floodlit drive, nor the three-storey Georgian façade. (I wouldn't have turned a hair at mock Tudor, but this was a surprise: it reeked of money and taste.)

I now regretted choosing the pink leather gloves with black ribbon ties, the black satin bodice and the pink suede mini-suit. It would have been perfect to impress the university Peter, and the riotous clash of colour with the plant's red leaves was meant to highlight my disdain for all things brash. But there was nothing brash here.

A valet took my keys at the steps and drove off over the gravel in my car. I was met in the capacious hall by a row of staff who took both my coat and the offending plant before offering me champagne. I knocked one glass back and took another. The house was alive with people.

To my right I could see a grand room with a huge fireplace around which beautiful people stood, chatting and drinking. To my left I could hear noises of many more in what must have been further reception rooms. At the top of the grand sweeping staircase in front of me, a girl trotted across the landing giggling followed by two expectant-looking young men. As I glanced up, two more girls, arm in arm, came in from the direction of the garden and headed up the stairs. There were other stranger sounds too, somewhere far off, which mixed with the noisy mêlée. I was too busy drinking in the scene to think about what they were, but they added to my uncertainty.

I was even a little nervous.

I took a deep breath to steady myself, but was rescued immediately by the welcome shout of Peter. He appeared in a bathrobe, a stunning black woman holding on to his arm. She kissed him knowingly on the lips, smiled at me and slunk off up the stairs. Not the wife I expected, either. The air was heavy with heat and perfume, and the smell of warm skin.

'You look as if you need a swim,' he said, and kissed me fully on the mouth. I could smell the girl's musky perfume on his face. He led me out through a wonderful orangery, where I noticed with surprise that many people were scantily clad and others totally naked. We passed a rather portly middle-aged man in the corridor who wore only a towel slung over his shoulder. His penis swung magnificently between his thighs as he held a hand aloft in greeting to Peter as he passed us. I pulled off my gloves and jacket as we walked along and thrust them on the nearest chair. Whatever this was I felt I needed to be a spectator for a while and for that I needed to blend in: that meant far fewer clothes.

We arrived at a wing of the house that revealed a vast grotto-like space with a long curving infinity pool. Water spilled, seeped and oozed lasciviously over its own edges, while a copious stream fell from a rocky outcrop at the ceiling. A fine curtain of spray rose from the stone floor where it landed. The steam, rising from the water, was lit theatrically from below. The space itself was cavernous and shadowy. There were about six couples in the water – others lounged in the rocky recesses on long couches.

Peter casually indicated the changing space behind the waterfall. Not at any time did he stop chatting amiably – about what I can't remember, my attention was elsewhere, everywhere else. As we passed by everyone's eyes would fall upon me, assessing me. It was slightly shocking, but in a delicious way.

When I reappeared, naked beneath a towelling robe, it took me a moment to locate Peter again. Then I saw him in the pool talking to two gorgeous couples. He hailed me, holding a drink aloft for me with that broad welcoming smile I knew so well. 'This should remind you of old times,' he said as he handed it to me with a kindly grin. His friends turned to smile at me – hungrily. I felt a surge of excitement fill my stomach. Who knows what will happen next? I thought and sighed inwardly. I let my robe fall to the ground.

The water was incredibly warm and the mixture of champagne and heat began to create a vaguely euphoric sensation within me. I began to relax in their company. All four were older than Peter and me, and surprisingly similar in looks. All had jet-black hair slicked back flat against their perfect skulls. Perhaps they are Spanish, I thought, realizing that it was becoming increasingly difficult to remember what I was thinking about. There were small strong currents in the water eddying around me; some even felt, momentarily, like the touch of a hand or the stroke of a finger. One of the girls was sitting on her partner's knee and, as she talked, she rocked backwards and forwards a little. As the warmth inside me mounted, her movements became more comforting, and I found myself mimicking them with my hips. A current of water lapped provocatively between my legs.

The two girls began to kiss each other. Not with light, tender kisses but with open-mouthed, saturated fervour. I glanced at Peter but he was engrossed in conversation with one of the men. Not so the seated support of the girl next to me. His expression had taken on a calm intensity and his body undulated in small and smooth snaking movements behind her as he pulled her back into his lap. The girls continued to lick, bite and kiss each other and one of them began to whimper. The men were all smiling now and began to encourage the girls with words of persuasion. Peter stretched his arm around my shoulder and gave me a reassuring squeeze. He had nothing to feel anxious about. The feeling between my legs was more pronounced and I looked down and was intrigued to discover that it was actually caused by another hand.

Ah – I thought . . . but I couldn't quite harness my mind to finish that thought . . . but it didn't matter. I had a flashback to Peter's phrase 'reminder of old times' as he passed me the glass. I felt suffused with happiness, my skin alive and sensate. Rational thought was distracting, so I surrendered myself happily to sensation.

Something long and silvery swept past me, under the surface, stroking me slightly with its wake. I turned slowly around to watch it pass but it had vanished. I scanned the water then raised my eyes to see a couple lying under the sluicing waterfall. Their naked bodies were drenched and, as the girl rose and fell on top of her partner, her brown hair seemed to pour over him like a sheet of molten chocolate. I stared at them for a second or two until my reverie was broken by the emergence of a long silver form from the edge of the pool. It rose, spilling water from its sides, and transformed before my eyes from fish to a pale-limbed girl in a silver swimming costume. She seemed oblivious to the long low moans beside her. She climbed out effortlessly and moved straight towards a table, where she picked up a small white towel and began to dry herself quickly and efficiently as she walked. She shook her head, causing iridescent drops to fly from her long pale hair. I was captivated by her independence from the scene. Who was she?

Where was she going with such purpose? I found myself inexorably drawn to follow her and pulled myself out of the pool as she passed into the shadows.

I entered a long corridor behind her. Her body was tall, taut and athletic and she swayed slightly as she moved silently, leaving long watery footprints on the varnished floorboards. She turned abruptly to her left into a flagstoned hallway. She reached up amongst the heavy mass of coats that hung beside the door and pulled down a white fur jacket. She slipped her long arms into it, shrugged the high collar close around her chin and stepped out into the night. I watched her hurry across the parterre. Snow had begun to fall. A warm yellow light shone out over an archway and she scurried into the dark tunnel and disappeared. Like the rabbit in *Alice in Wonderland*, I thought.

I realized that I was cold . . . and naked. I hesitated for a second as the chill air cleared my mind a little, then I stood on tiptoes to heave down a long brown fur coat for myself and let myself out into the swirling snow.

As my eyes became accustomed to the dark passage under the archway, I saw a welcoming light spilling from an open door. Inside, a long wooden table groaned with an abundance of cold meats, fruits and cheeses of every description that suddenly made me aware of how famished I was. I skipped over the threshold and the noise of the party burst about my ears as I found myself in a large old kitchen full of the smell of food and wine and warm bodies. The people's laughter was rich and infectious and I pushed myself happily into the throng. As I walked around the table, greedily filling my plate, faces turned to me in expectation, but this time I returned their smiles. Hands reached out to stroke my coat or my belly or my breasts as I passed. I felt sensuous and ravenous.

There was a slight clearing in front of the fire and I squeezed forward to see what drew the rapt attention of the crowd. There, reclining on a long sofa, was a large woman holding forth with a ribald story which she punctuated with loud guttural laughter. She gesticulated with an ornate goblet of wine and, with each eruption of mirth, fat crimson drops splashed on to her swollen breasts and rounded belly. She was magnificent – a female Bacchus. As I watched her perform I toyed with a ripe pear. It was engorged with juice and its taut smooth skin threatened to split open at any moment. I stroked it absent-mindedly as I watched her, imagining what it felt like to be surrounded by all that flesh.

The crowd pressed together and all I could see around was a sea of smiling faces until my curious gaze alighted upon a young couple behind the odalisque. They were fully clothed and seemed detached from the rest of the crowd. The girl was petite and pretty. She smiled and nodded as she listened to his animated talk. She seemed about to take her leave when another man approached her from behind and began to fondle her breasts. It was extraordinary – both the spontaneity of his move and her acceptance. I felt a pang of envy and a corresponding tightening of my nipples. She smiled a secret little smile to herself as he nuzzled into her hair. Then he lifted her skirts and entered her from behind. Her former companion leaned forward and took her face in both hands, kissing her deeply on the mouth. As her second lover's movements became rougher and more demanding she had to brace herself against the wall, pinning the first with her mouth and upper body. His hands moved down between her legs. She twisted slowly and sensuously into her enthusiastic lovers. They were amazing to watch, not least because they were enjoying each other so openly. The heat began to rise between my legs. As the pounding grew ever stronger, she threw back her head and I saw how her perfect little white teeth dug into her bottom lip. They were rising to their task now and I could see how close she was, and she bit her lip and breathed deeply to stave off the moment for as long as possible. Her lover continued to drive into her and at last she opened her mouth – I could only imagine the sound she made, drowned out as it was by the rest of the hubbub. The throbbing between my own legs became almost unbearable and I wanted badly to feel him inside me, grinding into me like that. I bit jealously into the pear as I watched, when suddenly she threw herself back into him and the fruit exploded against my tongue. The juices dripped down my hand and chin as he climaxed inside her. It was awe-inspiring. I wiped the juice slowly with the back of my hand, and sucked my fingers thoughtfully. The girl turned and leaned back against the wall and they all laughed together for a moment. Her face was alive and flushed with excitement and she said something and giggled and they all hurried out of the room.

I followed them with my eyes, then my heart leaped as I recognized the pale fur-lined form that passed through the doorway before them. I took up the chase once more.

The corridor was blessedly cool after the heat of the kitchen. I looked left and right and saw the long white legs disappearing around a turn in the passage. I felt a sense of rising excitement, wondering where I might end up this time. She led me to a winding flight of stairs. I crept up, following the sounds of the creaking wooden treads above me. I quickened my pace, hampered by the long coat I still wore, but when I emerged onto a quiet landing there was no sign of my rabbit girl.

I glimpsed through several doors in my quest to locate her only to find empty bedrooms. Eventually I stumbled across a room in which a young man with foppish looks, wearing nothing but a tie, pirouetted slowly round and round on a big brass bed to the encores of several attentive onlookers, most of them male.

I continued my search along the passageway, until I came across a closed door from behind which emanated earthy animal sounds. I tried the handle and an extraordinary room opened up before me. It was a sex playground. The walls and floors were covered in leather and from the ceiling hung a long black swing on which a pair moved joyously back and forth, propelling themselves through their ferocious coupling. They looked crazed and joyous. Their eyes rolled with each dip and thrust; their vocal lovemaking filled the air. The lower level of the room was empty and separated from a raised dais by a long bar which displayed a bewildering array of sex toys. The dais was partially curtained off with long black silk drapes, from behind which came the sound of someone begging piteously. I began to creep towards the sound, shocked and fascinated, when I noticed the girl. She was sitting in a tall wicker chair watching the suspended lovers. One leg draped over its arm and with both hands she was penetrating herself slowly, monotonously, with a large dildo. She would let it rest against the mouth of her pussy momentarily then push it in as she arched and strained against it to the rhythm created by their gasps and cries. Dip, thrust . . . dip, thrust . . . dip . . . their exalted sounds rose, as did her moans, and she stared fixedly into space, lost in her own masturbation until at last, echoing the other lovers, she climaxed long and hard. The swing couple fell into each other and as their pendulum swayed slowly beneath them they made copious sighs and fell about each other laughing. The seated girl looked about wildly and shuddered again as she withdrew the dildo and fell back into her chair, sated and sleepy. The noises from behind the drapes rose against the silence to become full-blown pleas for relief – I tiptoed through the room, to discover the source. It felt like I was entering a forbidden zone, but I was eager to see if my imagination did justice to the scene.

I peeped around the curtain to see several people in this strange stagelike space. They were all dressed in tightly stretched black leather, which constrained their bodies. I thought again about the feeling of holding the ripe pear. And indeed, as I watched, a masked character pressed a pinioned and gagged woman against the wall with a gloved hand. The woman's head was forced to look up to the ceiling and, with painfully slow deliberation, the front of her leather bodice was unzipped until a plump breast burst forth like an overripe fruit. She jerked and writhed in ecstasy beneath her bonds.

The air resounded with harsh words given like orders. It was intimidating but my curiosity just wouldn't let me leave . . . I needed to take it all in. Another woman was completely bound and kneeled at the feet of another who held her head aloft with a leash. At a bench a woman lay on her belly, her hands shackled to the floor on either side. She wore a full-length leather catsuit from chin to toe. Her partner leaned over her and reached between her legs to peel her zip back, revealing her crotch and buttocks. He penetrated her vagina with lubed fingers, making circles with his thumb on her perineum. The look on her face was one of pure transport. And as he began to insert a black leather butt plug she came with hoarse animal sounds rising in her throat. For a split second silence hung over the room and I turned to find that the players in the lower room had exited. The swing hung expectantly waiting for new players.

I felt pressure in my bladder so left to find a

bathroom. I soon found one within one of the empty bedrooms and I quickly trotted through, relieved at having found one and also at having a chance to gather my thoughts. I stared in the mirror at my image. I looked comical standing naked in the oversized fur coat – something like a gangster's moll. But I was proud of my body and I turned to reassure myself, stroking my nipples, which jumped to attention. I was ready for action.

When I turned off the light and unlocked the door I was startled to find that the room was now in darkness and I could hear the sound of muffled voices. Immediately, I pushed the door to again and peered through the small gap. There in front of the window, with the pale moonlight on their skin, was the pale-limbed girl and a beautiful black lover. I could only see him from behind but it was impossible not to admire his powerful buttocks or his muscle-clad back. She had changed, and now wore a pale lamé dress that shimmered like snakeskin. It only just skimmed her pussy – a fact he took full advantage of now. He pressed her back into the window casement, stroking and caressing her between her legs, then lifted her against the wall. She wrapped her legs around him and sank onto him with a sigh. I didn't know who I wanted to be most: they were two of the most beautiful people I had ever seen – had ever wanted immediately to fuck. I pressed the side of my forehead against the doorjamb and, taking great pains to control my own noise, I put a hand between my legs to touch myself as I watched. He was strong and lithe and rode up into her with ease. Her head rolled as they pitched and bucked together, her long pale fingers digging into his black skin. I rubbed myself harder and faster, causing waves of euphoria to swirl inside me. She abandoned herself to him and sank her face into his neck; her pale hair fell about him as her cries grew louder and more urgent as he drove orgasm after orgasm out of her. My muscles spasmed and contracted as I lost sense of my surroundings. I quietly closed and locked the door and dropped, spent, to the ground. I shut my eyes until I judged it safe to come out.

By now I was eager for company, so I pressed on. At last I heard the sounds of many voices rising and falling in a faraway room. I found myself at the entrance to a huge picture gallery and paused to get my bearings.

The space was chill and almost empty but for a huge ice sculpture in the form of Rodin's *The Kiss*. The doors to the balcony were wide open and a few snowflakes drifted in to melt on the bare wooden floor. I felt glad to still have the coat on and pulled it more tightly around me. Laughter and conversation echoed into the space from a room beyond. I was drawn again to the sound.

As I passed the sculpture I saw the pale-limbed girl. She held out a long arm from her shimmering sleeve, slid back to reveal her alabaster skin. In her long fingers she held a cube of ice to the nipple of a bare chest belonging to the man I had seen her with earlier. They spoke in low collaborative tones. Then, noticing me staring, they turned calmly towards me. I blushed deeply, realizing how stupid I must look. The girl smiled and continued to speak again in hushed tones I could not decipher, but she looked me directly in the eye with a gaze of cool interest as she let the ice slide down the middle of his chest. His perfect stomach muscles contracted beneath the stroke. I smiled weakly and hurried on.

After the chill of the gallery encounter, the warmth and buzz of the noisy room was a welcome respite. The air was thick with smoke and sitar music, the tables were decorated with marijuana plants and revellers lay all around the darkened edges of the room on piles of thick kilim cushions. I realized everyone was watching a blond couple in the centre of the room. He was sitting on the floor arching his back while she caressed and kissed his swollen erection.

I felt a tug beside me and looked down into the broad smiling face of a girl lying prone on the floor. A long mass of red pre-Raphaelite curls covered her naked torso. She proffered up a small hand-rolled cigarette and beamed at me. I beamed back and she patted the cushion beside her, so I slipped out of the fur and spread it out in front of us. She laughed delightedly and wriggled onto it so that we lay on our bellies together, feeling the silky smooth pelt below our skin as the sweet acrid smoke curled around us.

Before us, the couple continued their display. It was a hypnotizingly adept performance: she licked him lightly, rubbed her lips against him, then along him, while he twisted and moaned above her. He ground his hips up to meet her and she sucked the tip, nibbled his head, then took his full length deep into the back of her throat. My cunt felt plump and wet. Then my prayers were answered when a welcome palm began to stroke the back of my thigh. I spread my legs but I did not care to look to see who the perpetrator was – I was too engrossed in the show in front of me.

The blonde girl raised her head slowly, and I could imagine how the ridges of his cock felt to her tongue. She let the tip pop from her mouth and took him in both hands, squeezing him tight. Fingers slid up inside my swollen pussy and began to stroke and fondle me.

The girl who was twisted beside me rolled so that her head rested in the small of my back. I could tell that she was touching herself. It felt wonderful to be pinned down by her as she began to make small mewling noises and the hand between my thighs began to whip up a frenzied rhythm inside me, around me and through me. I turned my head to the side to admire her and saw a swarthy young man slide in from behind us to suck her astonishingly erect nipples. The hand between my legs began to alternate fast and slow circles around my clit. The couple before us moved inexorably, blind to the heat which rose in the audience around them. The girl slid her hand up and down his straining cock, taking him into her mouth and releasing him again. Then she slowly began to rub him between her full breasts. There were sighs behind me as the deliciously corrupting hand felt me clench my muscles. The redhead began to roll and whimper, pushing me down. The pace at my pussy slowed, but became harder and more intense around my hub of pleasure. I buried my face in the fur below me and groaned.

When I looked up, the performers now grappled each other and writhed in a powerful embrace until he managed to turn her onto her belly and she tipped her backside towards him so he could at last enter her. He bore into her from behind, sliding his cock in and out, tormentingly slowly, gripping her buttocks until she squirmed and moaned and began to shove herself back upon him. He brought down his palm on her buttock with a dull slap, then stroked her, then slapped again. I winced as I felt a long deep scratch along my inner thigh, then just as quickly the pain was soothed by a warm tongue. As the slaps resounded, so my mystery hand alternately dug burning paths into my skin then licked the offence away. The effect was instantaneous and the inevitable began to rise inside me. Fingers penetrated and scratched me, an unknown mouth licked and kissed my thighs, and the long tresses of the pre-Raphaelite slipped over my back and buttocks as the cries and moans around us penetrated the air with increasing urgency. I let my face fall again into the warm fur and gathered the pelt into my fists as light exploded inside me and I heard my voice from a faraway place cry out long and hard. I curled up below the coat between a knot of arms and legs and hair, and slipped into a dream.

I woke up feeling warm and happy and a little bit stoned. I looked around me to find the redhead asleep, entwined in the arms of her lover; much of the audience and our star performers had gone. The room purred with happy sleepers. I sat up to gather my wits, still feeling a little bit fuzzy, when I saw the pale-limbed girl crossing the room. She had shed her snakeskin and was completely naked now except for a thin silver chain that lassoed her slender hips. She carefully picked her way over the recumbent bodies and cushions with the precision of a Lipizzaner. She saw me and held my gaze for a second. As she passed she shook her proud head slightly and her long and tousled mane of silver hair fell about her smooth shoulders. I knew it was for my benefit, but whether merely for display or for enticement I couldn't tell. I had to follow. I had to know. I folded the discarded fur over the sleeping friends and left the room.

As my head began to clear, the previously mellow feelings were superseded by a pang of disappointment and irritation. The evening had been a protracted foreplay session. I now needed consummation. There was nothing that would satisfy me other than some long hard penetrative sex, and yet again I found myself wandering the corridors of this strange and magical party alone. I needn't have been anxious, for my pale chimera led me to the burning heart of the party.

The noise and heat and smell of sex hit me first. I stood at the threshold of a room that was a writhing mass of bodies. There were couples on couches, on the floor, even on a large golden throne in the middle of the room. It was wonderful and I needed to join in.

I hesitated for a moment inside the door, wondering what my first move should be. At my feet, a small dynamo of a man grasped a honey-blonde by her ankles and, manoeuvring her legs over her head to support his rigid body, he penetrated her slowly with his incredibly long shaft. She smiled up at me and I felt that familiar thrill as she did so.

The sounds of climaxing rose all around and mixed with groans, sighs and entreaties. There were mouths on cocks, mouths on breasts, mouths on pussies. There were girls riding high, girls being pounded doggy-style, girls on girls, girls on boys, boys on boys, couples, threesomes, amorphous groups of sliding limbs and tight embraces, searing kisses . . . The room dripped with passion and lust.

I wandered about like a sleepwalker until strong arms pulled me down and I found myself face to face with the magnificent black man I had seen earlier. He smiled and spread my legs. He kneeled between them, his hand on his cock. 'Touch yourself,' he commanded, and we moved with synchronicity, looking into each other's eyes. It was slow and intense and I moved to cup him as his balls tightened and rose up to his body, and he spurted a jet of semen across my belly. He fell forward upon my thighs and began to idly smear my juices around my folds until I was begging for more. He rolled closer and gently pushed his tongue inside and kissed and lapped and persuaded, taking me to the edge and back again, until I shook and cried. At last he moved up my body and, pinning my hands back beneath his strong arms, he slowly pushed his magnificent weapon inside and we bucked and strained. Stray hands and mouths of the invisible people around stroked and touched us as we rose together, until I felt part of an endless and indivisible knot of writhing, screaming, wailing lovers.

The heat of my body melded with the heat of the room and I slept momentarily. I woke to feel two mouths suckling at my breasts. A third clamped itself to my burning, aching pussy and lapped and licked until I was drained of every drop. I wriggled and squirmed in the delicious torment and felt hands grip my thighs, turn me over and over, pull my hair, as I was penetrated again and again until light and heat pulsed up through my body and my poor abused pussy was racked with orgasms, while numerous unknown lovers emptied themselves inside me. It was an excess of pleasure I had never encountered before. I dragged myself giggling and sighing to sit against the edge of a pile of cushions and fell back exhausted. I had to stop.

I awoke some time later feeling my body scratched, bruised and assaulted; my spirits delightfully liberated. The party continued about me but I had no more to give.

It took me a while to locate the pool again to retrieve my clothes. The water looked cool and tempting, empty as it now was of bodies. I plunged in, feeling the waters soothe my abused but happy skin. As I swam to the end of the room I heard the deep tones of a familiar voice. It was Peter. He lay on his side, lovingly stroking a recumbent woman's hair as he spoke. They were both swaddled in soft white towelling robes that looked soothing and very welcome after the night's excesses. I swam to the side and greeted him.

'Ah,' he said, and laughed at the look on my face. 'I knew you would enjoy yourself.' I didn't need to say anything, he knew me too well. 'But how rude of me!' he said. 'I haven't introduced you – this is my wife, Anna.' And the pale-limbed girl beside him sat up and smiled. 'If it wasn't so late I would ask her to show you around. All this is Anna's idea.' He gesticulated expansively and kissed her tenderly on the lips.

'Oh, not to worry,' I said. 'Perhaps I could see more next time?' She and I exchanged a complicit smile.

'Yes,' she said, softly. 'Next time, I promise.'

VI

I AM THINKING ABOUT YOU

I am in my bathroom holding a mirror to my pussy. I examine its folds, stroking them and watching them swell with expectation. It is not markedly beautiful and yet, in this shallow world in which beauty is paramount, what is it about this part of a female's body that is the ultimate allure to men . . . and some women? It is the source of life . . . and more transient pleasures. It is sacred in many cultures and yet its name is often used to cause most offence. It never ceases to learn new ways of stimulation – and it harbours the strange little mound that is the epicentre of a woman's sensual rapture. The more I come to know it the more I am in awe of its power.

It is Millennium Eve, a quarter to nine in the evening. The time demands some quiet contemplation and reflection on our lives – what we are, who we are. Below me in the street the crowds are already thronging. The world resounds with hope. All that anticipation of euphoria, the expectation of the moment, not of what will follow. It is like the pursuit of orgasm.

Thus I have an arrangement with you, my love, that we will come together, literally, at the stroke of midnight. It stimulates our sense of adventure that we will seek to experience *le petit mort* at precisely the cusp of the new century. I have to work later and you are at a party thrown by friends who do not know of my existence. We have sworn to achieve our aim while leaving our friends and colleagues unaware of our temporary absence. You will excuse yourself a few minutes before the appointed hour with the pretext of bringing in more champagne, and we will then have no more than five minutes together, probably less, to achieve the perfect orgasm – with the added frisson of being caught, or overheard, or missing the moment.

You are my soul mate, my collaborator, the co-explorer of my erotic landscape. We could not have let the opportunity pass us by. You may not realize that I also have an arrangement with another man to text him at midnight with the not-so-erotic, 'Are you coming too?' so that his phone will vibrate with the message and his wife will be none the wiser. I know it is lacking in poetry, and certainly not something I would usually agree to, but I have made an exception to allow for our own millennium challenge.

Normally, I demand a less prosaic scenario before I agree to become involved. I am excited by theatrical possibilities, by precise planning, by complex strategies. I need to be able to escape the confines of routine. And I love spontaneity. It is a rare quality in these modern times. What is it about the modern world that eschews all that excitement? What happened to the knee-trembler, furtively snatched in a darkened alleyway? Where are all those lovers, fucking alfresco, that our parents' generation predicted in the sixties? Surely the need for safe sex hasn't dampened our ardour – one can still be taken doggy style over the office desk by someone using a condom?

I am confident of my sexuality. I know what I want and I know how to get it. It is something you and I share. But there have been many men who have helped me explore the boundaries. I have found that those who seek out sex with equal ardour most often fall into four categories.

There is the successful alpha male, controlling and assured. They often mistake sex for intimacy. Sex with this man is always proficient, but can be less fun for the female if the element of risk is always missing. With them I like to suggest role-play in order to introduce the erotic element that comes with shifting power play. The Courtesan or Slave Owner are just two of a plethora of excellent characters for this effect.

The commitment-phobe will seek out sex with equal ardour, but they are often tired of their conventional lives and many yearn for a secret life. They often have predilections that their friends and intimates may know nothing about. They may like a good spanking or to be dominated. Or they may just like to have sex with strangers, or in strange places – vanilla style.

The adventurer is a particular favourite of mine – I love risk takers and rule breakers. But you cannot rely on them because they always put the pursuit of excitement above loyalty – and they can be selfish, volatile and immature. However, their exhibitionism makes them the perfect swinging partner.

Then there is the narcissist who seeks sex as comfort. I avoid them where I can. Sex with them can be a fantastically intense experience, but in the end it is all about them, and although they put women on a pedestal they are ultimately disappointed in us – either through jealousy or the belief that we don't match up to the their loftier ambitions for our character. They can also become stalkers. I once knew an artist who broke this mould, but then again I didn't sleep with him, he just paid to watch me masturbate or have sex with other men, and indeed one time a particularly orgiastic recreation of an eighteenth-century print he had once seen, with multiple partners.

I check the time; it is still only ten o'clock. An hour and a half before I have to leave to meet you.

I run a deep bath laced with rose-water and lavender oil. The steam pervades the room and my reflection in the mirror slowly disappears. The image of my pudenda is still clear in my mind, and as I wait for the bath to fill I languidly explore my sex with my fingers, reminding myself of its topography, its hidden secrets. As exciting as our assignation will be, it will be all too short and I now find the opportunity for extended foreplay while I think about you. The bath is now run but I am not ready to enter.

I place the thick, soft towels on the floor and lie on my back with my feet raised on the edge of the bath. I slide two fingers of my left hand inside myself while my right index finger circles and flicks my clitoris and the entrance to my vagina. I arch my back and throw my head back and begin to squeeze my pelvic muscles, imagining that I am milking your particularly long and rigid shaft. I visualize its ridged structure piercing me, so engorged is it, and even growing in stature as it approaches the inevitable. I feel my climax approaching and imagine your balls colliding with me in mounting urgency. My fingers are slippery with my excitement now and they move faster and harder until my shoulders and hips begin to shake involuntarily. I arch harder and push against the bath until even my hips leave the floor and a deep guttural moan escapes my open mouth.

I close my eyes and think of . . . nothing.

As I sink into the warm water, I think again about our plan and wonder how many orgasms will ring out at the same time. It's an awe-inspiring thought – the whole country resounding with the same ecstatic resonance.

I wash every part of me, checking intimately for any stray follicle that may have plans to disobey my strict aesthetic. I am not an adherent of the Brazilian school, but I believe vehemently in the 'semblance' of the natural look – however hard one must work to achieve the most visually pleasing 'untended' appearance.

I dry myself vigorously, buffing my skin until every inch is smooth and silky. I now rub the oil, paying special attention to the areas that your mouth and nose and fingers will come into contact with later. I dab it on my pulse points and under my breasts, knowing that as the heat begins to emanate from our embrace the heady scent will mingle with the smell of our sex.

I brush my hair and tie it up loosely with one clip – so that I can release it for you.

I open the box of lavender silk underwear that I have purchased specially for the occasion (and for the fact that the cups are intended to rest just below my nipples – a pleasure for the wearer and the viewer).

I choose this particular dress because it clings to my curves in a way that I know turns you on. My nipples will also become very visible through the fabric. Although, of course, you may not have time to notice these finer points.

The high-heeled shoes are sculptures in their own right. They lengthen my legs, enhance the curve of my spine, increase the rounded mass of my buttocks.

Then my face – I attend only to my lashes and my lips. You don't like too much make-up.

I am ready for you.

I survey myself in front of the mirror. Imagine how you will see me.

I am now all anticipation. Eagerly looking forward to your embrace, impatient to achieve the ecstatic union of two bodies through which we can transcend the boundaries of our humanity . . . for that perfect moment.

Transience? Of course. That's the essence of pleasure. We're not talking of lasting happiness. For that I have a cat.

The door closes behind me.

EPILOGUE

I AM WAITING

Are your eyes still closed?

I am still waiting for you.

I will meet you at an apartment in town. Go there in your mind now.

You arrive a minute early. Walk up the steps to the door. You wait to press the bell.

Look about you. Really sense what you are, where you are. Why you are here. Embrace the moment. Say to yourself, 'I am here, now. This is really me, in this place.' Prise yourself from your daily stupor. Awaken your senses.

We both know why you have come. But don't think about that now. It's not about the sex – yet.

Focus on a small inanimate object – a screw in the bell plate, a leaf on the step, something you would not normally notice. Give the inconsequential a consequence. It will become forever associated with what is about to happen.

Still all your rushing thoughts. Prepare a quiet place in your mind where you can internalize the whole experience. Experience it corporeally. Live only in the moment. Take a deep breath. Notice the temperature of the air as you draw it into your lungs. Be aware of the carriage of your body. Prime it. I will want a visceral response – later.

You are now ready to enter.

Ring on the doorbell. Listen to your heartbeat as you wait for a response. Notice your mood. Are you tense? Are you excited? Are you anxious? Relax. I will let you in.

Ascend in the lift. In that expectant moment as you rise to meet me you wonder what you will find. Don't. Don't think. Prepare your mind as a blank canvas.

You will stop at the door of the apartment. You will look for a method of entry – a bell, a handle, a buzzer – before you realize that the door is ajar. I am expecting you. Of course. I am ready for you. You will hesitate, but this is the last time you will do so. Once you cross this threshold it will all begin.

But it has already begun.

You enter the apartment. You are in a small but welcoming vestibule. It has soft shadows. Your eye catches a small object. That too will become part of your memory. You are vaguely aware of an ambient scent (it's cedar, but you don't know that yet – you will remember only later). It speaks to you now, though; it makes you feel like you belong.

You linger for a second. Then, fleetingly, you are anxious. Whose home is this? You look through the open doorway and to your relief see that the room before you is large and airy and empty . . . almost empty.

There is a large bed. It is strewn with crisp cotton sheets and throws of different textures, and pillows and a large bolster. Everything is white. It is neither made nor does it appear to have been slept in. It has the potential to be both cool and warm. You know it is extremely comfortable.

The bed draws you towards the room. You step through the doorway. The ceiling is high. There are three tall windows to the far right. They give out on to a view across the roofs of the city. There is one window across the street at the same level. (We could be seen.) Long curtains dress each casement. You notice them billow slightly. A window is standing open. (Will we be heard?) You notice the quality of air . . . again.

The walls are white – the floorboards too. You walk into the middle of this white cube. The room, you think, is like a stage. You turn around slowly, surveying the whole space, and you see the chair. It is black and tall with a leather seat and a high leather back. It stands alone. It seems sure of its position, sure of its purpose.

You like that, don't you? You hadn't noticed it before.

But there is something else you haven't noticed. Behind you. I am behind you, waiting for you to become aware of me. You will notice – and your heart will jump.

Neither of us moves. Neither of us makes a sound. But you will sense me watching you. You will know that someone is penetrating you – with her eyes. You know now.

You spin to meet my gaze. Your pulse quickens. Our eyes survey each other, secretly, without showing they are doing so. There is a mutual recognition of attraction. There is an instant physical connection. We both know that.

We must prepare ourselves. Shed the trappings of our daily life before we enter our fantasy. Before we can explore the boundaries of our consciousness. Before we can truly lose ourselves.

I am stripping for you. Here are my creamy shoulders appearing out of my shirt. Here are my breasts . . . and now the lines of my stomach, the strong muscles clearly defined. I do not show any hesitation. I know what I am doing.

I am naked now, except for my lace thong. I turn away from you, hook my thumbs into the fabric and slowly slide my hands down the edge of my buttocks and thighs. I have to bend over to lower them to the ground, to step out of them. But you like that, don't you?

You move towards me but I turn sharply and motion you to stop. Not yet.

I walk past you, out of the room. Where am I going? What are you supposed to do? But I am back now – with a blindfold. I secure it around your eyes. Unable to see, you need to be led to the bed – where I undress you.

We are now both stripped bare, here on this stage. But I have the advantage. I can see.

Tell me. Do you want the curtains open? Or closed? Do you want to be seen? I close them – this will be our secret. Should I close the window too . . . or let people hear you moan? I leave on the light – I want to be able to watch our show.

I stroke you from your breast bone, slowly down to your pubis. Quietening you. Think of nothing. Notice only your breathing.

In. Out. In. Out.

I want you to relax every part – before I reawaken it. Breathe deeply – let go.

Imagine your body, lying here, next to mine. Feel how heavy you have become. Now allow yourself to become flooded with warmth – from your hair, down through your cheeks, your mouth, your tongue, your jaw, your neck, your shoulders, your chest cavity. Think about your arms, your wrists, your hands and your fingers. Listen to your breathing. Let the flood pass down into your torso, your stomach, your pelvis, your buttocks, let it flow through your legs, your ankles, into your feet, your toes. You are warm; you are heavy. You are waiting. Your body is an empty stage. Breathe deeply.

You are ready.

Can you sense me yet? Inhale carefully; try and catch the smell of my warm body. Can you feel how close I am to you? Can you hear me? What am I doing?

I am waking your senses. I am stroking your fingers. I am running my fingers down your body, up your thighs. I am brushing the soles of your feet, sucking your toes. Feel me, experience the sensations more clearly than you ever have before. With every touch I am lighting your body.

Try to anticipate my next move . . . but you can't, can you? That's my tongue, moving softly up your body. Your body is burning.

You flinch. It is ice, held in my mouth. You didn't expect that, did you? It's encircling your nipples. Running up your inner thigh. Imagine how cold my tongue would feel on your cock.

I am astride you now. Kneeling on your hands.

You can smell sex. You don't need to see to know what is above your face.

You can hear me breathing. You can hear my hands stroking down my own body. You can hear me touching myself. Now lick me. Taste me. Can you taste how excited I am becoming? Can you hear that . . . that I . . . want . . . to? No, not yet.

I am kissing your thighs. Licking you. Stroking you. Nuzzling you. Your hands are free – touch me. I have you in my mouth, sucking you firmly, now teasing you, licking your tip. Feel it. I stroke your perineum, cup your balls, rub you between my breasts. I suck your nipples and hold my pussy above you, pinning you down. Tell me what you want? I won't let you move until you tell me your innermost desires.

This is your fantasy – tell me who you want me to be. Do you want me in costume – what role do I play? Do you want me as your slave, or your voyeur? How do you want me, from behind, so that you can pull me on to you? Do you want me to sit on top of you and ride you until you expire? Do you want to be caught? Tell me – tell me what you want.

I can writhe and I can dance but I don't yet know my role in your production.

Anything is possible . . . on the stage of the body, in the theatre of the mind. Who do you want?

I have removed the blindfold. The room is now in

darkness except for the chair, which is bathed in a spotlight. I am sitting with one leg raised, circling my clitoris with one finger. Waiting. Waiting for you. Will you come to me?

Here we are.

Embrace me; embrace the moment.

Enter me. Yes. Your hands and shoulders are a fortress. Discover what 'fuck' really means. Yes? Tell me. Who do you want? Yes, you, with your hands that pull yourself into me.

Who do you want? Yes, yes – you whose lips that press upon me. Yes – tell me, you whose teeth are biting me. Yes – you whose shaft impales me.

Who . . .

Yes.

Do . . .

Yes, yes.

You . . .

YES!

Want?

?

I am
I can
I will
I could be
… anything you want me to be …
you just need to persuade me.

WHO DO YOU WANT?

who_do_you_want@hotmail.com

Other books in the series:

Agent Provocateur: The Secret Life of V

ISBN 9781862057470

Further reading:

Agent Provocateur: Secrets

ISBN 1 86205 720 6

Agent Provocateur: Confessions

ISBN 1 86205 726 5

Agent Provocateur Exhibitionist

ISBN 1 86205 714 1

www.agentprovocateur.com